BOLDEST ACTION SAFEST

Flotsam and jetsam, from those days of bedlam
Now washed up on a foreign shore
Present civilian life a bit mundane, ...a bit bore

The axle grease on the *khukri* has long run dry
A bit of moisture ..stays at the edge of your eye

Recce troop Jongas growling @2 AM in a QRT (Quick Reaction Team)
Or waiting for a Zil lorry repair by dawn @ the FRT (Forward Repair team)

You can buy a 20/30/60 year scotch today
But long to clap your hands in the Mess and shout 'Koi hai ?'

You can walk in to any club, any lounge, unmolested
But try that at night at the ammo dump - and you will be contested

Choicest cuts of meat, cheese rain like manna from above
They can't hold a candle to a jawan's proffered mess-tin brimming with love

No longer immersed in Patton, Guderian and Burma campaign
Guess we all have made our Faustian bargain

Shade of a T-72's sprocket wheel in 45 C heat is no big deal
Rolling out the bedroll on a tanks' radiator... that thing can heal

He's been standing a post, all shivering and cold,
When you were imbibing Dutch courage, acting tough and bold

So don't ask a veteran 'Did you kill anyone out there ?'
Coz its always easy to kill.. but VERY tough to spare

CHAPTER 1 : DIGGING IN WHEN IT COUNTED

It was 4 PM and the dusty fine silt-sand rose lazily in the merciless May heat that enveloped the Shivalik foothills on the Uttar Pradesh/Uttarakhand border, somewhere in Saharanpur District. This is the training area where the Indian Military Academy (IMA) trains its mid-level Gentlemen Cadets (GCs) in domains such as mountain warfare. Our Usman platoon, a part of Naushera Company, stirred into action, swatting away flies and insects, and waiting for the evening tea-truck to arrive.

The night before, we had crossed many wide, rock-filled seasonal streams, called 'raos' that descend from the Himalayas, which mostly carried little water for most of the year, but when they did, they were raging torrents. Pre-monsoon showers had begun in the area, but that only added to the sweltering humidity that could make a water buffalo drop in exhaustion.

The night before, the rao had been relentlessly stormy as it got runoff from the showers, filling our boots with mud, and making every step a duress.

'Oh Addy... ! you have not dug the trench since lunch ! Capt Vijayant is the duty officer and you know his nature !' I said exasperated at my happy-go-lucky 3-man trench partner, Rajesh Singh Adhikari - appropriately shortened to 'Addy'

'Paro, relax, ho jayega', (it will be done) he replied, shortening my surname in equal measure. Addy was a dreamer, who had drifted into the Academy, strumming a guitar and having a good time in his college days. Ebullient, stylish, and charming to the core, he was a product of the famed Sherwood school in the hills of Nainital.

He could have had an easy entry into a corporate career, joining legions of nameless Doon/Sanawar/Sherwood alumni who either found power as faceless bureaucrats in the Indian Administrative Services (IAS) or any of the Central/State govt services,, or made money as bankers to the rich, or some years later, be a startup founder had things gone in a different direction.

But it was in Naushera Company, that our paths crossed, with me coming from the National Defence Academy (NDA), and he coming as part of the graduate entry, straight into Dehradun's Indian Military Academy (IMA). The IMA is organized into 4 Battalions, named after Indian Generals, and has 3 companies each, named after famous and historical Indian battle victories - in WWII and post-Independence conflicts. It has trained many Service Chiefs, of various nations, including those of India, Pakistan and other nations.

He and I were room-mates for a couple of days, but I needed a non-smoking roomie, so I opted for a solo room, when that opened up in an adjacent building. We remained on good terms as a combined course of ex NDAs and 1st term Direct Entries trained in the 2nd term.

Unlike the nameless friction -in early days at least - that can plague the dynamics between ex-NDAs and direct IMA entries, Addy attracted people to his persona. He was an easy-going soul who got along with everyone, with his tales, guitar skills, and canny ability to imitate anyone he interacted with.

In fact, his mimicry of our bete noire Company Commander berating us had everyone in splits, including the said Coy Cdr, who in turn encouraged him to join his own Mechanized Infantry Regiment.

Cut to present ... circa May 1993.

I and another GC cursed not-so-subtly under our breath, grunting and heaving in our sweat soaked overalls as we dug the trench. A healthy fear of front-rolling in the stone-filled river bed, kept us going in the still heat. Much to our chagrin, we saw Addy return from where the Company stores were dumped - smiling with his guitar in hand.

'This is one Mughal-era army which marches on its music'

'If the Pakis attack your post, I am sure you will serenade them not with guns but with your guitar'... our comments flowed freely as being short handed left us on a short fuse.

Unperturbed, Addy strummed an old Hindi movie song. 'Ude jab jab zulfein teri'. This was our course's song, and one could trust Addy to bring a tune to life. I and my fellow digger exchanged knowing glances, and shook our heads, as we resumed our battle with the rocky trench.

Was this how it will be in our lives, where people like Addy will coast, and people like us will struggle for the next 20 years ? Time will tell.

'You bloody *bh@*gi* ! Get rolling' ! came the staccato bark from the Kohima company location, from the rocky ridge located next to us. Capt Vijayant had arrived with his signature cussing and free flowing wrath at GCs in close proximity to him. Politically incorrect vernacular was the hallmark of the Captain, as he effortlessly chastised a hapless cadet, labelling him as one of the sweeper/cleaner castes.

While our hands dug faster, there was no way we could have turned a knee-high hole into a respectable trench to mount the light machine gun (LMG). The afternoon's cholley-bhaturey lunch, a rare treat, was threatening to come out via whichever way it could egress the body.

Soon it was our turn.

'What the hell is this sorry hole in the ground ? Is it a urinal ???' asked the Captain, wearing camouflage outfit, with stylish riding putties wrapped around his ankles - and the half-orange and half-blue ribbon of Vir Chakra, India's 3rd highest military award, visible prominently above his right tunic pocket.

The Captain was a legend unto himself. Hailing from the DOGRA Regiment, he was a veteran of combat in the 80s in the rarified, icy barren 22,000 ft high Siachen glaciers' ridges, where he had repulsed multiple, relentless attacks on his posts by Pakistanis, fighting till his bullets ran out, as his men perished under ferocious artillery strikes. As a last ditch resort, he picked up an 84 mm Carl Gustav rocket launcher (RL), and fired rockets on to Pakistani attackers, till they were repulsed with casualties, and turned the tables on his attackers. For this spectacular act, he was awarded the Vir Chakra (VrC). He was a tough, no-nonsense officer, who prided on cutting no corners in training, and was held in awe even by his peers and superiors, given his combat record.

'No...no sir, we are digging a 3-man trench" came our weak response.

'It's almost sundown... the enemy is watching you and is radioing your sad position so that his mortar team can wipe you off the face of this earth !'

Is this what you are going to fight with ? Come out, you clods.. get bloody rolling'

Resigned, we came out, looking for a little bit of cool mud to ease the body as it rolled on its back. Time to be ready to sweat from every hole in the body, and whatever else came our way. As we got on our haunches, the Capt's demeanor, and voice, changed on seeing Addy.

'Addy, good to see you.. Are you a part of this lot ?', he inquired solicitously, smiling.

'So what's holding up progress?' he asked in a dulcet tone, none of the edge of 2 min back in his tone, as if he was talking to a long lost buddy. Thinking on his feet, Addy made up a story about being given that location 2 hours back. The Captain grunted, and visibly relaxed.

'See you at the campfire... you guys ARE having one right ?' he inquired.

That was interesting. While he had his cadets, it looked like he was thinking of visiting our campfire.

As he walked away into the darkness, we could not believe our luck.

'So much for learning battlefield skills, when your guitar can do the talking.' someone wise-cracked, though general relief to see the Captain walk away was palpable.

Soon sounds of carnage rose from the adjacent Poonch Company location. Just like us, hard rock and terrain meant the 3-man LMG trench being dug there was no good, and choice epithets bellowed from that direction, followed by hasty sounds of spades hitting hard earth. We tried to ignore the carnage's sounds and sights.

As dusk fell, the Captain returned, with a hip-flask giving him company, as he picked a boulder to perch on, and we gathered like starlings under his care. We had left IMA almost 24 hours back, and surely deserved a relaxing campfire, and a hot meal.

Addy began playing tunes and songs on his guitar, and soon a handful of officers came over, cupping their beverage of choice. It was as if the Pied Piper of Nainital had come playing his tunes. Hard-boiled Captains who had fought insurgents and Afghan jehadis in Kashmir, silently gathered and sat on boulders, listened transfixed as Addy sang and played soulful tunes as the evening melted away into darkness.

On occasion, talentless ones like myself, added to the chorus, singing off key,, but otherwise it was all Addy's show. We survived that night, but always wondered if Addy would be able to hack it when the chips were down, and he was facing a tough situation... and God forbid, combat.

6 years later, we would find out about his abilities - in the national media -, almost to the day.....in May 99.

As a Mechanized Infantry officer, he went on cross-attachment with an Infantry unit, the GRENADIERS, deployed in the Kashmir Valley to fight counter-insurgency. As Indian patrols sent to reestablish vacated mutually-vacated snowy ridges - as per an unwritten decades old understanding - they disappeared, with no one the wiser. Bad weather, faulty communication equipment, snow storms, were the usual causes when radio contact with a patrol could be lost for days or even weeks, and since they were equipped for survival, it was not found to be an unusual eventuality.

This time, however, the missing patrols of the JAT regiment caused concern after additional days were gone , and then without a trace. Inquiry with local shepherds revealed the presence of outsiders, visible in the snowy, alpine pastures, in the direction of Pakistani Kashmir.

As the initial patrol was 'recovered' - mutilated and hideously tortured after 3 weeks of custody, with their bodies handed across distant Attari border near Amritsar, the mood turn to deep rage at the betrayal and custodial killings, in violation of the Geneva Conventions and prevailing code of conduct amongst soldiers. The Indian war machine began to crank up. Despite the short notice, the till then, slow-to-move juggernaut of the Army began spinning and throwing more and more troops into the Kargil mountains - rarefied heights where the enemy was dug in, prepared and waiting since March.

It became evident that while India was lulled into a peace bus ride that March, the wily Pak general Pervez Musharraf, had launched a plan to cut off the reaches of India's Ladakh region from the mainland, and forcing India to negotiate 'concessions' over Kashmir.

Short of acclimated troops from the plains of Indian mainland, orders came to bring forward all available units from the nearby Kashmir valley, as it would take weeks for troops from far flung cantonments to reach the battle area, located in the northernmost reaches of India.

Addy was soon deployed with the tough 6-footer GRENADIER soldiers, earning their respect and ably leading patrols to re-establish supremacy, and engaging in skirmishes and shooting wars.

Before one particularly risky mission, he received a letter from his newly married wife. Instead of reading it then, he is said to have folded it away, planning to read it in peace when he returned from a patrol up the mountain ridges.

It was not to be. Over he went across the frontline, and into harm's way.

On 30th of May, as his men were tasked with evicting the dug in enemy from a forbidding feature known as Tololing Top, Addy and his troops came under formidable fire from the enemy above. Facing near vertical ridges, grabbing footholds, he fought like a man possessed, leading rocket launcher attacks. As the opposing soldiers got closer, no quarter was given, or taken. Hand-to-hand combat ensued, where Addy killed 2 intruders, and in the process getting shot and severely injured - his anguish heard by men as he clutched his radio set.

He kept guiding his men, till his last breath.

Another Naushera company coursemate was now directed to get to where Addy fell, and resume the charge. Addy's death galvanized the men, and after ferocious hand-to-hand combat, came victory, and the headline 'Indian troops capture Tololing' in the Times of India.

It would be a few days before his body, and those of his fallen comrades would be brought down as they had been booby-trapped. Even in death, the fighting went on.

On his final journey, the entire city of Nainital gathered to bid him farewell… and his name became a legend - in the Army, across India, and on the lips of every school kid of that generation and beyond. Today, his name is inscribed at the National War Memorial, and a site of revered pilgrimage for any person in our batch passing through the vicinity.

On your 26nd anniversary, all I can say is that it's been a privilege to be in the same half-dug trench as you, Addy-boy.

CHAPTER 2 : WHAT RESTS UNDER THE JAP CAP ?

Of all the classes and lectures I have slept through, it would be fair to say that it is pretty much impossible to nap in a bayonet fighting class. The National Defence Academy, Khadakwasla (NDA), located near Pune covers this skill in great detail for its final term - the 6th termers. The class is a part of curriculum for the Army cadets, and is regarded as a crucial skill, with theory taught in class, and practicals and graded tests in the field.

The NDA - a unique premier, tri-services training Academy that turns 18- 19-year old boys into future officers, follows a tri-services modelled organization structure, with groupings modeled from respective services - the Army, Navy and Air Force. (There are no Marines, as similar roles are taken up by Special Forces, assigned to each service).

At the NDA,, the Squadron (Air Force) is the core entity, housing about 120-odd cadets, across 6 terms, and that's what a cadet is assigned to. The Battalion (an Army unit like organization) is what's formed by 4 such squadrons (e.g. 1st Battalion, with Alpha, Bravo, Charlie, Delta squadrons), and a Division, a squadron-specific entity, 4 of which go into a Squadron, is the smallest unit of organization. In essence, each course of about 300 cadets is organised into Division-> Squadron->Battalion-> Academy type of an organization.

The service training begins in the 2nd half of a cadet's 3 year stint at NDA, as respective training teams begin imparting their own training to the cadets. The Army Training Team (ATT),, after careful selection appoints some of the most tactically strong, battle experienced officers, Junior Commissioned Officers (JCOs) and Non-commissioned officers (NCOs) for cadet training. Around 70-75% of cadets per course are a part of the Army intake, and would then hone their skill for a year at the Indian Military Academy, Dehradun, from where they are commissioned into their respective choice of arm (eg Infantry, Armoured Corps, Engineers) or service (Army Service Corps, Army Ordnance Corps etc.)

Carried out on vast open ranges, with sheds called stands, captions such as 'Victory is still measured on foot', and 'One bullet, one enemy' are emblazoned on camouflaged boards. Cadets get dispersed as per their respective Squadrons, where some of the most ruthless, combat-trained NCOs and JCOs run the classes, under the supervision of a Colonel Saito type (of 'Bridge on the River Kwai' fame) Weapons Training Officer (WTO).

Machoness drips from these perpetually-camouflage wearing, hands-on-waist, mustachioed alpha males, who have taken the God-given task to whip lethargic cadets into future officers in the Army, who would be worthy of the respect and leadership of the troops they would command.

We as juniors, would aspire to don the well-starched Olive green dungarees, put on the pouches and paraphernalia of the FSMO (Full Scale Marching Order/Outfit), and, with a flourish, mount a bicycle, with the rifle magazine resting on the front handle bars, and the barrel on the shoulder. Little did we know that behind the mud-caked olive green dungarees, and tired smiles our seniors wore as they returned, they masked a complete rogering ('shellacking' is the word Obama uses in such scenarios) they underwent at the weapons training classes and firing ranges. On most days, they would simply retire to their cabins, skip the evening games, and just call it a day.

One headed to a full day schedule for such classes, where lunch would be packed, stuck into one of the pouches, water bottles filled, for later consumption. Mercifully, the bayonets would be sheathed at that time – to prevent any Darwinian outcomes en route as we rode in 4- or 6-man squads, rifles balanced precariously on the handlebars.

Since a bayonet fighting would obviously require a target, a straw dummy, propped up by an NCO who wielded a long, thick, bamboo serves as one. Both the target and the NCO manning it, look equally menacing. The NCOs do not conceal the fact that even though in another short 12 months, they would be saluting you, at the moment, they pretty much disdain the notion of any authority from a 'green behind the ears' cadet like you.

That indifference/disdain between the NCO and the cadet (mutually refer to each other as 'saheb', indicating the respect due and given by both parties), is masked by a genuine desire by the NCOs and training team to have the cadets learn all the skills they would, when deployed on the border, or the Line of Control in Kashmir. That aspect only dawns, when one becomes an officer, and realises how overlooking the need to appoint perimeter scouts could lead to an ambush and casualties, or how critical the role of road-opening parties (ROPs) is in counter-insurgency areas.

These lessons are written, and learnt in blood, and formalised in a kaizen-like constant improvement process, where a slight distraction, or a less than robust check of a boundary wall could lead to overlooking a terrorist getting ready to shoot a burst at you and your team.

Most of the instructors - Officers and NCOs alike - are posted after acts of conspicuous gallantry, and actual courage in the face of the enemy. A deputation to a service Academy is a matter of pride for any Army unit or battalion, as such spots are coveted and indicate the proficiency in their skills. The chosen instructors (men, as of 90s, but now many women are a part of the training) would have direct, frontline experience – officers and men alike – who have fought off Pakistani attacks on their posts, or braved avalanches in the Nathula area bordering Tibet/China, or those who have fought with domestic and foreign insurgents such as the Liberation Tigers of Tamil Eelam (LTTE) or the myriad groups present and fighting in India's North East states (The Seven Sisters).

These are men who have seen colleagues fall into crevasses below, as the enemy cuts off the rappelling rope while climbing up on oxygen-deprived slopes above 20,000 feet, and go above and beyond the official curriculum to train cadets in what will keep them in a dominant position versus the adversary.

In this world, where Infantry is still the queen of the battlefield, skills such as close-quarter-combat (CQB) and bayonet fighting are regarded with samurai-like reverence and dedication. This is a stripped down, mano-a-mano form of fighting, where you are face-to-face with your nemesis, who is similarly equipped, and charged up with notions of religious or ethnic superiority based on his carnivorous diet and tribal invader Pathan heritage. Such battles have been fought on razor-sharp mountain tracks, in steamy jungles, or on 30-inch wide animal trails as you come face to face with the enemy at a short notice.

So, here we were, during the monsoon season, in July of early 90s, with the full force of a Sahyadri mountain driven rain beating down on us. The rains in Maharashtra are akin to a proverbial deluge, as the monsoons come charging in from a bathtub-like lukewarm Arabian sea, and rises up the slopes of the mountains and dumps water by the bucket. Rain pours in sheets and covers everything. It trickles down to layers and body parts you think are safe from any such probing, and then it sloshes in your not-too-robust boots.

Amidst all that soaking, we were lined up, awaiting our turn at the row of dummies, which still looked in better shape than us. As part of the attack drill, a sequence of intricate rifle and body movements are expected, as you lunge at full pace, with the skilled NCO wielding a long bamboo, as the dummy's weapon, with flourish and glee, poking you repeatedly and ensuring that the dummy is protected.

In this muggy monsoon heat and humidity, our WWII design Jap caps are usually put aside on the ground. An interesting feature of these caps is the 'snake bite kit' that is attached to them – consisting of a near-rusted shaving blade, some twine and twigs. The theory being that once bitten by a snake, the wound is supposed to be excised by a buddy, using the blade, and the poison sucked out, and a tourniquet applied.

I am pretty sure that while the snake venom would not kill you, the subsequent tetanus surely will. I am now told, the said kits are now rendered obsolete, as proper medications, specific to the snake species, are now available.

After an hour of duking it out with the dummies, we were dispersed. Like a beaten army, we packed up our soaked gear, put on our caps, and rushed back to our respective squadrons. Packed meals awaited us, as we had to then go to another set of hills where the days' classes on tactics, fieldcraft and weapons training awaited us, taught by officers who wouldn't tolerate any delay, tardiness or anything less than perfect uniform, called 'turnout'.

While we were riding to these classes, my buddy Sam, felt something move around the brim of his Jap cap, somewhere above his right ear. While he was still riding the bicycle, and balancing the rifle, he did not think too much of it, patting it down firmly. A short while later, something appeared on the brow of his cap. Thinking the snakebite kit had come loose, he pulled at it – and found himself holding a suitably agitated snake.

All bedlam broke loose, as Sam and the snake were staring at each other on a bumpy bicycle still going full clip, pedals moving, legs pumping, and tail wriggling. A crash inevitably followed, and both were free of their mutual loathing, in the overgrown undergrowth. The snake must have been disturbed by the melee of that morning's bayonet fighting,and coupled with the incessant rain, decided to make himself comfortable in the warm confines of Jap caps lying on the ground, picking Sam's cap.

When the time came to disperse for the day, the cap, and the snake coiled in it were swooped off the ground and worn. Breakfast must have been eaten in a short window of time, and it was not for another 15-20 minutes that the 2 found themselves staring into each other's eyes.

So it fell upon us to help pick up Sam, his bike and equipment, and get him going. At this time, cadet appointments like Sargeants from other squadrons are looking to 'check and punish' juniors from other squadrons, so it was best we put pedal to the metal, even if the pedal, and the foot were close to being broken, and the head hurt or worse, bitten.

Where the snake went, no one knows, but like us, it too was pretty shaken up, and did not want another encounter with humans.

Sam is now a Senior officer, but anytime we gather, the memory of that encounter always lightens up the mood. I am sure he regularly checks all caps he wears on his now bald head.

CHAPTER 3 : 'LIMELIGHT' OR 'PICKPOCKET' ?

Just out of the right corner of this bucolic picture of NDA's vast Khetarpal parade ground, lies a white marker, dedicated to Limelight, the Adjutant's horse from years past. It reads :

'In memory of Limelight, a faithful charger who knew this ground well'.

The marker emphasises the deep and historic links the Army has with animals - going back to days of Marwari horses like Chetak, ridden into battle by Rajput King Maharana Pratap, to more humble mules of mountain artillery and bomb detection dogs used in Kashmir valley. Unlike these revered and adored animals, Limelight never stole the hearts and imagination of cadets - plowing a tough to plow furrow in the asphalt of a parade ground so vast, a MiG 21 could land there.

And while there were other stellar horses, like the quartet of Clydesdale type pack horses that haul the ceremonial buggy, that brought the Chief Guest to the Parade ground, the singular heart capturing feel undoubtedly belonged to another beast - Pickpocket - A shaggy dirty blonde beast with an unruly mane and a tail that never got combed due to his 'unique' characteristics.

Possessed with the kind of ample girth -'beam' in naval terms - the kind with which Roman chariots formed passages that led to the measurements of the modern railway gauge - putting a saddle on him meant running the risk of getting an iron-shod hoof to your face.

He was never fond of being ridden ... that too in rainy weather and the open fields of the Glider Dome whose vast savanna like terrain had him go 'frisky'. He just wanted to be left in his stall, munching on his bag of oats and chana gram. Riding with unskilled, frenzied cadets was never his idea of a career, for which he drew full rations for.

With a propensity to kick and scare away any novice or even experienced rider, Pickpocket quickly got a fearsome reputation. In fact, such was his level of dread, that cadets would flat out refuse to ride him - preferring to rather get Restrictions and Extra Drills, for disobeying orders - than ride him.

And the protocols followed by the riding 'ustaads' didn't make the experience either pleasant or have one take up riding as a sport. In the obtuse way of imparting horsemanship by making things difficult, and also in the name of overcoming fear and building 'officer-like qualities' , one had to go 'under and over' the blanket clad, saddleless horse, a few times to warm up, much to the puzzlement of the beast whose nether zones one came face to face with many times - as thick mustachioed cavalry instructors sized you up, making it clear they had more respect for the horse than you. Lady Mary of Downton Abbey would have quit her horse, had she visited NDA's equitation lines for her initial foray.

The riding instructors could have come straight from the set of a wild west, or Bollywood action movie. Most of them hailed from the dry, dusty, arid regions of Rajasthan or the tri-junction between UP-MP-Rajasthan states - with the famed bandit hideout of Chambal belt (of dacoity fame) being a common calling card for many of them.

True to form of making us fear the sport, these instructors had many a moves packed within their bandoliers and riding puttees such as -

(a) bringing PickPocket ONLY to the freshmen batches of 3rd termers, new to riding, and unaware of his girth, dimensions and notoriety.

(b) renaming him altogether with benign names like Rasool or Bahadur - anything but his real name so the rider would not bolt before the horse itself did. That would be like renaming Billy The Kid, or Wyatt Earp of the American Wild West, names like Sam Claxton or something similarly benign.

A year or so back, my Facebook feed had a picture taken by a coursemate showing a marker bearing Pickpocket's name among the departed equines- leading to both glee and just a tinge of sorrow. He had been given a tombstone akin to the noble steed that graced the parade ground, while never even stepping close to it.Comments such as 'RIP, you devil' flew thick and furious from many of those sent skywards by his hind quarters.

It was acknowledged that of all the horses in the paddock, Pickpocket ruled the roost - and lived and died by his own rules - probably kicking the vet who must have administered the lethal injection to him.

Comparisons to that WW1 mare's epitaph *'Here lies Becky the mule, who, in her lifetime, kicked 20 privates, 10 sergeants, 5 officers... and a bomb.'* were made.

But come to think of it, that's how humans live as well .... in life and in the workforce. Many amongst us are the 'Limelights' - doing their jobs, plugging away in relative anonymity, and upon retirement or demise, easily replaced by another Limelight, who is younger, cheaper and just as hard working.

And then there are the Pickpockets - never destined for greatness, but relishing their game of golf, their 2.5 hour workday lunches, their guffawing inappropriate-by-a-mile jokes at the water cooler. Behind closed doors, they are accused of spoiling the youngsters, and bringing down the culture of the establishment, a fact they know is true, deep in their hearts, but they would be loath to admit that.

IF motivated,... And that's a big IF ... and turned in the right direction, towards an objective catching their fancy, they would canter and then gallop at breakneck speed, hitting that sales quota for the quarter in one business meeting. But make them go through endless product training, and they will buck and storm out, yet turn around and pontificate on the finer aspects of that product that even the instructor wouldn't be aware of. Then they would snort and paw the grounds of the Glider dome of life, where the views are endless, and targets are ripe for taking.

Choose wisely. Either you are a Limelight. Or a Pickpocket

CHAPTER 4 : KARGIL WAR - THE SAGA OF THE VANISHING SIKHS

Two memories remain fresh in my mind from May-June of 1999, when India and Pakistan went to war over the icy wastes of Kargil in the state of Jammu & Kashmir. The war was a plan pursued by successive Pakistani leaders from 1948 onwards, spurred by a vision to 'wrest Kashmir from India, before the asymmetry between the 2 became insurmountable).

The first is this cover of 'Time' magazine, which shows the iconic 'Punjabi Mussalman' (Punjabi Muslim) soldier, grim faced, resolute, with a binocular in one hand, raised on grass-fed beef, and indoctrinated to be equal to 10 'daal (lentil) eating Hindus' in war. His other hand was caressing a dark barreled light artillery gun.

In the interview, the soldier is interviewed by a very sympathetic TIME correspondent, about his 'tough' job - shooting and blowing up red painted Indian Oil trucks plying on the snow bound National Highway 1A between Kashmir and Ladakh region, supplying and stocking up kerosene, petrol and diesel for both civilians and troops based in a region that would get cut off during the months long winters.

Each spring, the National Highway 1A (NH1A) linking Kashmir valley to the Ladakh region would reopen after a long winter. The highway passes through Zoji la , a high mountain pass, and Drass, the 2nd inhabited coldest town on Earth. Once the Border Roads Organization personnel cleared feet-high walls of snow and ice, supply trucks, carrying food, fuel, oil, and other essentials would be sent towards Ladakh in cowboys 100s of trucks long, along high, open mountain roads, visible from peaks surrounding them. Should there be anyone aiming at them from the heights above, they would be exposed and vulnerable to aimed fire - and liable to be easily picked off one by one - like a fox in a hen house killing chickens

In the interview, the soldier is relaxed, as he talks about shooting and blowing up defenceless civilian oil tankers, his task and aim made easier due to their bright red paint scheme, as his quarry lumbered up steep slopes, right into his field of view as he pulled the firing lanyard, unleashing a shell that would lead to a fiery death of the hapless truck crew.

Clearly, times were different then. Indian sensitivities mattered less to either the Pakistanis or their American backers that time - fed on the need to keep Pakistan safe due to its 'strategic depth' - a nebulous concept that has provided a lifeline to many a Pakistani ruler.. The fact that this was an act committed without a formal declaration of war between 2 sides, was not touched upon in the interview.

Historically, it is said that 3 A's rule Pakistan - Allah, Army and America (now close to being replaced by China), so if any 2 are aligned, then the 3rd ruler also falls in place, including celestial powers.

Till that time, the unwritten, yet honoured convention was for both Indian and Pakistani troops to vacate their frontline icy bunkers when winter sets in, and then re-occupy them once weather grew warmer in spring. No one encroached on any vacated position, and peace prevailed, as both sides watched each other from a distance, dutifully filing away reports of their day's observations. A soldiers' code of honour had prevailed for decades... till that spring of 1999.

Earlier in the 90s, when the Pakistani Chief, Gen Pervez Musharraf, was Director General of Military Operations (DGMO) of the Pakistani army, he had proposed the invasion plan to then Prime Minister Benazir Bhutto, to sever India's lifeline to Ladakh, and had found no support at that time.

But a few years later, with a more pliable, halwa-poori loving businessman PM, in Nawaz Sharif, the wily Pervez put it in motion, with no more than 4 senior Pak Army generals being aware of it, and keeping their own Air Force and Naval Chiefs in the dark (A fact duly acknowledged by Pakistani authors such as Group Captain Kaiser Tufail's accounts, and other non-Indian sources.)

In early May, as Indian Army patrols sent out to check on the vacated positions disappeared, artillery shelling of border towns like Drass and Kargil picked up, and locations such as a TV broadcast station, along with an ammunition dump were blown by bombardment, the conflict picked up in intensity.

India, behaving like a slow moving boxer, initially took some hits, and lost precious weeks to marshall its resources, but by mid- to late-May began to throw everything at the intruders... which brings me to the second memory of that time.

At that time, I was working as a Systems Admin in HCL's Gurgaon office, during the days before it became the outsourcing and globalized Tech mecca it is now. The stretch of highway to Jaipur, on which Gurgaon lay, went past the then single-runway Delhi airport, next to whose approach runway was the location of an infantry unit designated for the airport's protection - the 8 SIKH infantry unit.

The tall, well built, lanky Sikh soldiers would be seen spending their mornings maintaining their area, and playing volleyball, as Boeing and Airbus passenger jetliners landed a few 100 yards away... at times, they would be ogling at the procession of buses of IT employees, heading to offices of GE and HCL and other tech companies.

Then...one morning, as if the ghosts had swung by, not a soul was in sight, except for one obviously-injured guy who was sitting under a tree, with a leg cast. The whole complex had a deserted look.

The Sikhs had simply vanished. I immediately realized what had happened.

The sole guy was recuperating, but the rest of the unit had been deployed. They had, almost overnight, drawn their weapons and ammunition, put on an Indian Airlines Airbus A300 and taken to Srinagar. With barely any time to acclimate to the heights, they were then progressively inducted higher up via Sonamarg, till they were in the theatre of war.

The unit was amongst the 100s that were pulled from the summer baked plains of India, taken up 1000s of feet into the juggernaut of mobilization, and launched into the cauldron of war. Hardened formations such as the 8th Mountain Division, already deployed in the Kashmir Valley, for counter-terrorism and counter-insurgency duties, switched mental gears, aligning with their motto 'Forever in Operations' and got back into their war-fighting role, deploying over the Zojila Pass.

By early July, after weeks of pitched artillery battles conducted by dug-in batteries of Swedish 155mm Bofors field howitzers, the time of reckoning had come. A particular saber toothed mountain peak that dominated the landscape and known as 'Tiger Hill' , became a last redoubt of the Pakistani infiltrators.

With razor sharp edges, it dominated the skyline, with kilometers deep visibility of the highway, allowing Pakistanis to call artillery fire on the road. To clear this feature, 8 SIKH, coupled with 18 GRENADIERS along with 2 NAGA infantry units led a frontal assault, ultimately battling hand-to-hand with the Pakistanis, some of them choosing to jump into the abyss, rather than be captured.

THe NAGA troops are a legend unto themselves. They are a couple of generations removed from head hunting tribes and formidable masters of the art of ambush. Till the 80s, these tribes themselves had battled accession to India, and after a peace accord, were now recruited as their own Army regiment.

Over the next few days, even after a ceasefire was announced in distant Washington by President Clinton, and Pakistani PM Nawaz Sharif, the battle raged on, as both armies fought hard to seize, and retain control of dominating features that would now realign the Line of Control (LoC). Alongside, the grim task of recovery and dispatching bodies back to their hometowns and units went on.

One day, the SIKH unit's soldiers were seen lined up in a 'hollow square' formation, with a few garlanded coffins in their midst. A Sikh prayer could be held over the loudspeaker. Some of those soldiers, who had played volleyball a few weeks back, now lay in plywood coffins. The same aircraft they watched arrive and depart, now brought their departed brothers in the cargo hold. Our entire bus turned emotional at the sight.

Over time, a lot has changed. India never left that part of the border unguarded, even during winters, choosing to raise an entire Division of 10,000 troops. When the firefights begin again, one tends to read about news such as a madrassa or a mosque being hit 25-30 km away, about how 'unprovoked Indian shelling led to death of a 14-year old girl'... It is always a child or a woman who somehow blunders their way around a terrorist hotspot, as collateral damage and has a rendezvous with a High-explosive shell, never a Pakistani soldier.

While the human rights and religious freedom guys go through their made-for-TV wailing sound bytes, what is left out of the story is that the same mosque or madrassa had been visited by a leading terrorist leader of the Jaish or another outfit... And in targeting them with a pin point 155 mm round laid squarely in their courtyard, we let the Pakistanis know .... that we know who they are hiding in such facilities.

That didn't change in 1999 - and has been the same in the May 2025 4-day conflict - Operation Sindoor, when any attempt to use sub-conventional warfare or revive insurgency - is met with a resolute, well defined impact detonation of either a rocket or an artillery round.

CHAPTER 5 : PART 'B' EXAM FROM THE DESERT

Late Mar is when the unofficial 5th season in the Armed Forces - Exercise season - starts wrapping up, as the Rajasthan desert heat slowly but surely reminds humans that its hot breath is never too far away. The process of deploying in the designated exercise area, which, on map, is 'supposed' to be bare desert devoid of human settlements, yet each year, more and more houses, unauthorised borewells and crops are seen, leading to troops being trained deeper in the desert.

Our induction for one such large exercise - Bhavani Khadka (Khadka is the sword of Goddess Bhavani), was memorable indeed. The Commanding Officer (CO), an intrepid cyclist, and his state-of-the-art Concorde Pro10 were a known face in the cantonment, and easily recognised as he rode dozens of km, nonchalantly from Nabha to Patiala and points thereabouts, and he thought of us deploying to the desert - via bicycles, as a great way to have some fun together.

So, along the lines of the Tour de France, a 'Tour de Punjab' was organised. The Map section got busy with milestones, bounds and other info along the Nabha-Sangrur-Bhatinda-Suratgarh axis, where we would later be picked up for a move deeper into the Exercise area ahead of Suratgarh. Pakistan's Fort Abbas is a couple of map grid squares away, and sand columns of advancing tanks are easily, and intentionally shown to the opposing forces - without any binoculars needed.

As a fresh-from-the-Academy 2/Lt , my name was right up on the list of cyclists. I commandeered a cousin's school going bicycle, and showed up - an assortment of Lts, NCOs from sports team and some hapless overweight JCOs press ganged into cycling. The ride along mustard and wheat fields, is bucolic South Punjab territory as the green melts into the gold of the desert.

As we rode along the eucalyptus-lined highway, and soon, the sight of us pedalling away on a busy highway brought fast-moving staff cars, and their occupants, to a grinding halt. The CO is a respected figure known for his deep domain knowledge, and once the Staff Officers relayed back about this 'induction by bike', in true Army fashion, tablecloths materialised, *pakoras* and *chai* were rustled up, and we got to meet Majors and Captains who, as students on professional courses, had been taught by the CO, and were now serving as Brigade Majors and Staff Officers across various formations. They effusively paid their respects to the Old Man, and gave us impromptu 'learn as much from him' pep talks.

Those who had the best deal were the ones bringing the tanks via train, as Officer Commanding (OC) Train, and we could at times spot their leisurely parallel move, while we snorted in the fine dust around Pilibanga. Soon, the sand became too overpowering, and the Tour came to a halt after a 150 km advance, somewhere before the deserts of Suratgarh.

So come Late Mar, the exercise wraps up, and everyone is seeking to go back to civilization, clean crisp bed sheets, and not eat food out of a mess tin. Plans were made by Capts and Majors around what movies they will watch, be with their loved ones (no, not the Officers Mess's Bar NCO), after the grand finale of a 72-hour non-stop combat advance exercise, implying the younger officers will be coordinating the return back. With the shortage of locomotives, rolling stock in 90s India, it would be April before we could realistically expect to show up back in our Punjab location.

There was also the *'langar gap'* (informal chatter) that the upcoming Part 'B' promotion exams for Lieutenants to Captain rank, will be deferred due to our exercise exertions. Fat chance of that happening, but hope lies eternal right ?

Besides, with us sitting miles from anywhere, the law exams, which need Military Law manuals, and the one on Military History, needed detailed study, and it was unlikely we could pass, without any prep time, after months spent in the desert. I had thrown in some fading Academy handouts from the Burma Campaign of WWII, and would read them while sitting in my T-72 tank, while waiting for the next move.

The radio set crackled, and in came a missive from the GOC -
'All Part B candidates must muster up at their exam centers on the due date. No exceptions'.

That set the cat amongst the pigeons. Red faces of Captains, Adjutants and others turned in our direction. Protests of 'In our days, the youngsters stayed back' could be heard in the field mess, which we wisely avoided, choosing to dine with the troops.

'Sir I am ensuring the men have the water truck available for a wash' was a good excuse.

But orders were orders.. And the seniors couldn't do much to change them. While most of us were packed off in relatively comfortable Jeeps and Gypsies (versus the suspension-less 3-ton Shaktiman truck some rode for 16 hours), some got to hitch a ride on an Antonov-12 transport plane to Chandigarh. One guy was picked from his tank by a Mi-4 chopper, given he was out of radio contact sitting on a 30r sand dune. Soon we found ourselves in a school building, sun-burnt but happy. I ended up clearing 3 out of 4 papers, causing some grief from a Capt whose tally was more modest.
A fitting end to a long drawn spring in the desert.

CHAPTER 6 : WELCOME YOUNGSTER !

Great leaders are those who make even the newest, greenhorn joining their organization, feel welcomed, and cared for. It's a lesson that's seen, and imbibed thereafter.

On this day, many years ago, the Passing Out Parade (POP) of the Indian Military Academy was mustered and ready to march in the pale sunlight of Dehradun's wintry morning. Admiral VS Shekhawat, the Naval Chief was the Presiding Officer.

As per custom, the NCOs of respective Companies had warmed up their contingents, so they could march in with aplomb and execute Drill movements with precision. This parade was special as we had received our choice of arms/service a short while back, and many were heading to the Kashmir Valley, and other hot spots, so this was the last time we were marching together - as one.

The Subedar Major (the seniormost non-officer rank), akin to Regimental Sergeant Major – marched up to the Adjutant, who was astride his white horse, and saluted - face to face into the steamy soaked gram smelling breath of the beast.

He saluted and said 'Brig Training saab is arriving'.

After the Commandant and his deputy, the Brigadier Training is the boss, at the Academy which has produced Army Chiefs across India, Nepal, Pakistan and Bangladesh. The training rigor he sets, is followed by the Chief Instructor and his legion of Directing Staff (DS) body of Majors and Captains, all of them with exemplary careers and 'courage in the face of the enemy'.

So his arrival sets the proverbial cat amongst the assembled cadets and officers alike.

Soon enough, the purring sound of a blue Ambassador staff car with a 1-star pennant approached behind us. A flurry of stamping of 13-nailed drill boots and salutations could be heard, as we stared impassively ahead. The shooting range had taught us that any movement attracts attention, and we all just wanted to get to the relative scrutiny-less safety of the Parade ground itself.

'Will the Officer commissioned into Hodson's please fall out?' came the assured, firm baritone. Officer - not Gentleman Cadet ! That sent goosebumps up my spine.

Oh wait ... That would be me. Again, it took me a moment to realise that would be me !

Here I was, commissioned into a very tradition-bound armoured unit which came into being during the maelstrom of 1857 War of Indian Independence (aka The Sepoy Mutiny), by a Major who was credited with ending the Mughal dynasty by executing the Mughal princes.

'Don't mess it up, they could hold you back if you screw it up !' a voice spoke inside my head, as the eyes of ~400 peers and seniors fell on me.

Trying hard not to stumble, I fell out of formation - gave one rifle salute to the Adjutant, an about turn, a brisk march, and another salute to Brig Training- who happened to be my Unit's Commanding officer not too long back.

'Congrats again youngster, here's something for you', as he brought out a silver badge with the unit insignia.

I was momentarily stumped.

Here, on a day where the national media, a Service Chief, countless officers and parents of our batch had gathered, and his presence would be needed at the saluting dais, he had made time to reach out, with a cherished, handcrafted insignia.

Recovering my composure, I accepted with solemnity, and fell back to my contingent.The Staff car drove away, and soon, we marched in - putting our best foot forward.

90 minutes later, during the pipping ceremony, I switched out the Academy peak cap badge, and put on the Regimental badge.Decades later, the cap is on my hat stand, the badge is secured in a bank vault, lest I lose it.

That lesson of care has stuck with me since then.

CHAPTER 7 : TATRA DOESN'T CARE

The leave plan of the dashing Captain of the Light Repair Workshop (LRW) , a paradoxically named body of engineers in the Armored Corps that repairs heavy tanks, was melting away like a vanilla cone in the Rajasthan desert. Exercise 'Bhawani Khadka' was on and Ambala based 2 Corps was revving up its warfighting muscle and tank engines across 100s of sq km near the Indo-Pakistan border, close to Suratgarh.

The frontline armored regiment had gone through collective training at the troop level, but during a 72-hour night advance as part of Combat Group (Regiment level) exercise, a T-72 tank had fallen in an unmarked well, the likes of which were popping up all over the ground, driven by water shortages in the area and rapid growth of population. Being unauthorized, they were not marked on the maps that were provided.

As a result, what showed as a vast vacant space on the map could be temporary fields, and the said unmarked, boundaryless wells, which could swallow up or significantly trap or damage a tank driven over it at night.

The Captain was recently married, and left his young wife back at the Unit. In the exercise area, he led by example, working 18 hour days ensuring the tanks were operational, and was really hoping to be back with his bride, rather than share a stone 'dhaani' (hut) appropriated by Captains and Lts & 2 Lts like me - all bachelors.

The kind-hearted CO must have approved his leave right after the CG level exercises, but then the Old Man was summoned back to Patiala for a conference at the Div HQ.

Now the regimental 'baagdor' (affairs) was in the hands of the 2nd-in-command (2 I/C).. that too, a 2I/C awaiting the results of his promotion to the next rank, and the future command of the regiment. Lambs have a better chance of a consideration in the African savannah than getting leave from a 2 I/C at such times.

The 2 I/C also epitomised the traditional Rajput warrior, being from a storied warrior clan, hailing from an aristocracy with their own citadel haveli (thikaana), where ladies are addressed as 'rani-sa'. He was a man of few words, and while kind-hearted, woe betide anyone who fell short of his expected standards in battle preparedness.

.. and our Capt was soon to find out how short he was going to fall in the tasking assigned.

His responsibility was to provide an Armoured Recovery Vehicle (ARV) crane that could pull/winch the tank out of the sandy well.. and a Czech origin, Indian-made 'Tatra' - a TAnk TRAnsporter to ferry it out (hence the name), that's actually named after the Tatra mountains in erstwhile Czechoslovakia.

And while the ARV had successfully pulled the tank out, much to the Capt's credit, the Tatra had a damaged set of screws that rendered it immobile. Without replacing the screws, the

Tatra couldn't move, and now he had another heavy, immobile piece of complex machinery to bring back on-road.

By the time the said screws would arrive, his leave would be toast, given that they would be special ordered and could be anywhere - Patiala, Ambala, Chandigarh... or points further south. The Capt spent the entire day seeking out the 2 I/C and trying to get his leave approved. He would beseechingly implore that 'He would be back before the screws arrived...' or 'He would chase them down to source and return with them.' Words that fell on deaf ears, to no effect.

None of them good enough for the 2 I/C to approve.

Things came to a head at the Officers Mess tent that evening. No sooner had the '*aabdar*' (bar NCO) poured the 2 I/C's drink, the Capt popped in front of him, and repeated his need to go on leave. We could see the 2 I/C shake his head, and turn redder by the minute... and then he exploded.

'I want to help... but Tatra doesn't care about screws !'

and then driven by exasperation and the heat came the words..

' if it doesn't get its screws... neither...' and then he stopped mid-sentence, as the import of completing that cause-and-effect dawned on him before the words left his mouth.

There was pin drop silence.

One of the irreverent Captains snickered...

Both the 2 I/C and the Capt stood frozen in a Mexican standoff, as the import of the words painted a vivid pen picture in the minds of everyone.

To his credit, the Capt recognised the 2 I/Cs inadvertent faux pas and gave a resigned head nod. Much relieved, the 2IC also smiled.. and the 2 of them moved to a corner of the tent, drink in hand..

An awkward situation was diffused.

Around midnight, as I was doing guard checks and relieving my tired driver from sentry duty, I caught a blur of the Workshop jeep, and the Capt with his black patka (bandanna) flying, heading towards the city to flag an overnight bus out of the area, and make his way home to his waiting wife.

'Get some magazines sir ....' was my shout to him.. and he didn't disappoint, returning with a wide grin on his face and 'magazines' pouring out of his baggage.

CHAPTER 8 : LANDLUBBERS ON THE ARABIAN SEA

Deep in America's rural Pennsylvania, are communities of Amish people, who live a 19th century lifestyle going back to simpler, pioneering days. They avoid technology, moving about in horse-drawn buggies, and working with their hands in furniture making etc. A life of Gandhian simplicity one would say. Among their traditions is one called 'rumspringa' (literal meaning 'jumping around'), which is a rite of passage for adolescents where they go to cities like New York, and have a good time, for a brief while.

The NDA has something similar.

Acutely aware that its tri-services training means that the Naval and Air Force cadets, post academy, won't need to fire a rifle, and the Army folks won't dip their toes in the seas as they head to 'Northern challenges', they arrange a trip to a fighter base for everyone - and a day on a sea going warship - a cadet level 'rumspringa' which would, in a perfect world, have us return with cans of Coca Cola, cheeses (this was the pre-liberalization, early 90s era).

Our rumspringa was a trip to Bombay Harbour, and board a ship that would go out into the Arabian Sea, circle an oil drilling platform, and bring us back, with some new found appreciation for our colleagues in white.

After this, most of us would be heading far away from the ocean, digging trenches in rock faces, at times under enemy fire in the Himalayas... So with this trip, we could see how the silent service members lived... What could possibly go wrong here....?

One crisp dawn, we piled on in our khaki 'walking outs' , our grey woollen berets at jaunty angles, starched trousers rustling about, for a pre-dawn departure from Pune to Dadar, a Mumbai train junction. As Army cadets, we felt smug and superior to whatever the 'Naval dopes' will put on display, by virtue of firepower, maneuvers etc.

Just the other day, we had been to a firepower demonstration by a KUMAON unit which had been one of the first to be inducted on Siachen Glacier, then on to the IPKF in Sri Lanka, and had just come back from the counter-terrorism grid in Kashmir. Watching Medium Machine guns and 84 mm rocket launchers fire with deafening roars was what it was all about...

What can the Navy show us to impress ? - we thought in our haughty foolhardiness.

We were to board a (then) newly inducted South Korean built Offshore Patrol Vessel (OPV) named INS Sukanya. The ship glistened quayside, in its battleship grey paint, and bristling with armaments, radar and communication pods and an onboard helicopter and had a new car smell to it.

One of the attractions of a defence establishment is its 'canteen' - which is like a US Post Exchange (PX), where, unlike the more mundane shampoo-soap-hair gel that one gets in scores of military canteens, these had (gasp) - assorted cheeses, beers, Sony walkmans,

Drakker Noir perfumes and other stuff. 6th termers past would decorate their cabins with these goodies and be seen as being 'on the program' and worth emulating.

Strict instructions were passed to not act like hooligans, and maintain decorum. Finer points were relayed to us - as in you salute the ship when getting on board and disembarking. That 'Officers don't go on liberty' (shore leave) like naval ratings, they 'proceed ashore'. We could see a senior or two, now midshipmen, in their spotless white shorts, talking an incomprehensible technical jargon, and scurrying about. Such a delight to see, considering I had only seen him in satin gowns in his last term at the Academy.

INS Sukanya was carefully eased out of the jetty, with Mumbai landmarks like the Gateway of India and Taj Hotel a stone's throw away. We were already dreaming of a naval reception, with damsels to bedazzle, upon return. The muddy grey black waters of the Colaba docks churned into a reluctant fury, as the ship pointed out to the Arabian sea.

Soon the sea spray was hitting us in the face, as the diesels roared into life. We could see the city skyline recede. About 5 km from the shore, the water color changed from muddy grey to a sparkling green, as it got away from the detritus of a densely packed metropolis.

But dark clouds hovered metaphorically over our fates.

The ship's Captain noted that the cadets were not much interested in the briefings his officers and crew were imparting. We were told to stiffen up. Lounging about and sunning ourselves on the deck like beached whales did not look wholesome.

The batch before us that went up to the ship's canteen had already raided all the good and affordable stuff. Word came back that those trips are no longer allowed. So much for shopping for the 'good stuff'.

Soon it was getting blustery topside, and we made our way to the galley for a lunch of chicken *biryani*. There were strict instructions for the disposal of bones, so as to not clog up the ship's plumbing, which was intricate and challenging to maintain even in the best of times. Lets just say that post-lunch an assortment of chicken bones found a way into the sinks and plumbing - as a final act of revenge by the birds, cast on those who had eaten them.

As the ship ran into progressively stronger waves, just consumed biryani lunch made a determined effort to rise to the surface. Soon, we were lined up en masse over the railings, throwing our guts out, much to derision and smirks of naval ratings, who were keeping an eye on us with pity and disdain. Gone was our swagger, our superior attitude. The lack of sea legs was showing as the ship headed towards the offshore drilling platform of Bombay High.

I went downstairs briefly, and was greeted by a strange sight. Our Cadet Captain, and a few other appointments had been press-ganged in the kitchen, picking out chicken bones from the sinks and other undesirable areas. What a shocker ! ... our eyes met, and quickly averted.

I had no desire to be rounded up like Putin's mobilization into finding bird bones, so came back up hurriedly. In silence, we waited for the trip to be over, longing to be on firm land. Gone was any desire to attend a naval reception, and meet the glamorous Colaba high society and talk about polo ponies ridden by young Army officers.

Our rumspringa had turned into a day-long bathroom session. We boarded the train back, not even picking up the dreaded 'packed dinner' and just found any space we could in our reserved coach. No one said a word, as the train headed back to Pune.

Never was the outing mentioned again. I am sure it comes up as those amongst us have risen to be ships and submarine Captains, and Brigadiers planning amphibious landings. But the jointmanship is best not tested on a heaving ship in the Arabian sea, but in richly empanelled Officer messes with dark paneling, upholstery - and darker beverages waiting to be imbibed.

CHAPTER 9 : BATTALION FALL-INs

Like a mother-in-law relishes breaking in a new bride after marriage,, like an Equestrian 'ustaad' (NCO instructor) takes pride in breaking in a new unruly gelding, and the hapless cadet astride it, the Battalion Duty Officer of the very first Battalion fall-in after a term break makes it a point to go after the 'swachhand' (free-spirited) 6th termers.

At the benighted hour on the reporting night, usually 2130 h, the new Battalion Cadet Adjutant (BCA), who, for the past 3-4 weeks, had been practicing his 'Batttaalionnnn Saaavdhan' (Battalion.. Attention !) commands all day like a rooster on crystal meth gets to come out on his own. His peer, the Cadet Captain adjusts and readjusts his tie pin and practices his about turns to give report to the Duty officer.

Come the hour, and the shuffle and loud stamping of juniors of Fox, Golf and Hunter squadrons comes into Echo Parade Ground. Fox had a particularly devious bunch of seniors - while standing, they would create a hollow cavity within which one of their juniors would be 'cream-rolling' (1 front roll, 1 back roll, zero displacement, zero noise) - during this entire process.

On one occasion, I was flying in from Delhi, and a kindly Battalion Commander and his lady wife on the same flight gave me a lift in their staff car, with me dismounting as the Capt quizzically looked and stiffened in the direction of the purring Ambassador car. Of course, I got punished for 'showing up late'... followed by 3 Sinhagadh hikes for 'travelling under my own arrangements'.

Such is life in the Academy.

An indistinct roar, and howl would arise from a flank... Looking up, one would be dodging steaming hot dollops of Maggi noodles and soup, falling to utter wastage mere feet from us. Capt Dhume had sniffed out a senior merrily cooking Maggi. After forcing him to eat boiling hot Maggi from the heating plate, he disdainfully flips over the mess tin and makes Maggi rain. The senior whimpers and rejoins his coursemates. Us juniors dare not look back... And so the legendary song of 'Dhume... *Galiyon me ghoome*' along the foot tapping lyrics of 'Tap tap tapori' would be born.

'*Phaccchhaaack*' came the resounding slap from Capt Kuber as a 6th term cadet gave some lame excuse for his tardiness. Pindrop silence prevailed again. As juniors, you are not to savor, or even watch a senior's sufferings. Pointing at me, and asking my name, he hollered 'How long back did you announce the fall-in ?' I had enough sense to just swallow and gulp. 'And where is Cadet so-and-so ?' he asked me.

'Sir .. he is on his way' I blurted.... 'You want to be a diplomat with me ?" he glowered. My steadfastness that night got me a couple of pals in the flank, and an endless supply of egg rolls from that point on. Better to face the heat of an officer for a moment, and end up victorious with 2 x 6th termers being issued as pals for a lifetime to hang around with.

'Don't call me sir' never sounded sweeter.

Much later, in the US, the phrase 'snitches get stitches' made complete sense to me.

5th termers who had coiled themselves in the squadron balcony cooking halwa would leap onto adjoining Ashoka trees and climb down as though they were performing climbing rope, 2nd class to rejoin their flock. The smart ones among them had gotten their friendly *sahayak* (attendant) to tip them off and unlock their cabins to make a catty escape. Woe betide someone found in the squadron when everyone had fallen in.

3rd and 4th termers would discretely unpack bundles of King Burger from the city, while standing motionless. They had been brought in by a sweaty junior carrying probably a dozen giant 'buffalo meat' burgers - hence the cheap price, which probably blocked their entire kitchen for a good amount of time.

A show of 'Rambo II' would be snuck in between and a mad dash on the local PMT bus to catch the last bus to Kondhwa from Deccan Gymkhana, and the burgers were there at 9: 30 PM sharp. Modern Doordash was inspired by those inveterate burger flippers.

To add torment to the general sense of despair of another 5 months ahead, the prevailing westerly winds would invariably blow gastric emissions from Fox denizens on to our hapless location. A wave of frozen repulsion would lash 2nd and 6th termers alike. On one occasion, so deep rooted was the aroma that a collective groan was let out - and the entire squadron promptly got called in *bajree* (gravel) order, and the SCC vainly trying to explain the sudden desertion of discipline in the squadron.

More insidious were the lip-smacking 'pak pak pak' sounds made by bored seniors, that would elicit suppressed squeals of laughter, and the ire and continued stand to by the Battalion Duty Officer (BDO), mystified as to where the sounds were coming from.

By that time, a healthy dose of self-inflicted masochistic pain is almost a necessary nightcap before bed, and it won't be fun if we were not berated by exasperated officers for our lack of officer-like qualities.... By continuing to extend this agony session for our seniors, we were showing our defiance, in that 'you can make our lives miserable, but you too will suffer the same.'

Those were the nights.

Chapter 10 : FORCES BETWEEN COURSES

Hierarchy in the uniform starts as soon as a cadet steps foot in the academy. You can find your classmate from schooldays, who cleared the exam an attempt or two before yours, and therefore be a term or 2 above yours (or below, if he was late in passing the UPSC entrance and the SSB interviews and Medical exam thereafter). Cadets also get transferred between squadrons e.g, if the report ('putting up' of a senior by a junior (snitching in present terms) leads to said senior be punished or lose a term, then the junior better not be seen in that squadron.... Ever.

Traditions, good or bad, follow cadets from their parent squadron. Mine was notorious for not letting juniors have evening snacks till they had completed Camp Rovers in 4th term, while as a 6th termer, one could be seen embedding 4 besan barfi pieces between your fingers, one for 1-4th term, and their own. The 5th termers now got 1 piece each. This 'just because now they could' left a long lasting sense of hurt and injustice... which promptly disappeared when your own turn at said privilege arrived.

A transferred cadet arrived from a pretty 'tough' squadron, one where rumors of brainwashing - dunking a junior's head in a toilet bowl, and flushing - was known to take place. Our squadron did not have this tradition. So one night, when the juniors were taken to a bathroom session - which involved ridiculously rolling through hot and cold showers, this transferred senior found himself carried away by the moment, and took a junior to a Western style toilet stall, trying to force the junior's head for a 'brainwash'.

The junior, who had been a boxer, was perplexed, then horrified, and upon realizing what was going on, in a flash, reached for a phenol disinfectant bottle lying there, broke it, and put its jagged edge at the neck of the now bewildered senior. The python was trying to swallow a crocodile, which was now threatening to rip out his stomach - and so the tables turned.

Pin drop silence prevailed .... His own batchmates intervened, not to save the junior, but to defend the fact that this was simply not, 'squadron tradition', and that 'he was not in his old squadron anymore.'

Others intervened, trying to separate them, ultimately coaxing the broken bottle and releasing the grip on the neck of the junior, in a choreographed move that would make Berlin's 'Bridge of the Spies' proud. None of this got reported, as both would have lost their term badges. But the smoldering dumpster fire of intra-course (see how I navigated the spelling there ?) persisted.
By the end of 3rd term, the dynamic between the courses usually hits an all time low. The juniors know that after 3rd term, they no longer have to suffer physical punishment, or lift

bicycles, or be made to front roll, and can only be made to report in various 'rigs' (outfits), as 4th term had its own privileges and physical chastisement was no longer applicable.

By the end of May, as Passing Out Parade (POP) practice is in full swing, the summer heat inflicts lanyard burn in your armpit, due to repeated left arm swing while marching with a rifle. The overall misery index is pretty high. One late afternoon, a usually mellow senior was making a bunch of us roll in the heat, due to our squadron's drill movements being called out for not being up to the mark, during POP rehearsals. Giving him a cold glare, I did a couple of slow front rolls, making my doubtfulness ample to him.

'Parjan...is this how you show reactions to a Corporal?' came the bellowing voice of our Battalion Cadet Captain, a Div Senior, who was observing this from his flank's bathroom. He trailed out in a loud guffaw, as he was our Div Senior, so was supposed to be protective, but his duty also wanted him to make sure the 4th termer administering it was not getting disrespected.

In a flash, I did 3-4 front rolls, reaching the edge of the Battalion area, in 1/4th the time of my till-then slow rolling rate. The Corporal himself was left behind, and could only grumble 'You couldn't show better reactions earlier ?'. My point was made, and he had dispensed his brand of justice, even though it was administered from high above. Scores tied.

A year later, it's the same summer heat, and cross country practice is going on. I am a Vth termer, and this guy is CSM. We had climbed up Table top, a hard patch that is tough to run during summer, and bogs you down in the rainy season in sticky black soil. I was doing my own leisurely run, when I felt a tap on my back. It was the CSM urging me 'come on.. V termers are expected to do better' .

Initially I said ' No sir, I will catch up'... (we are both running side by side). He again tapped, and made a snide comment about how juniors would look up to me as a 6th termer.
I didn't need any motivation particularly, as I usually was conserving energy, and made up anyway down the long downhill stretch that lay ahead.

But his tap, and smirk got me going... Using my God-gifted long legs, I picked up speed. CSMs usually avoid coming to practices, so he was a bit out of Cross-country shape. I could sense that in his labored breathing.

Now, he was in a *saamp-chachoondar* (snake and muskrat - where the snake can't eat a muskrat, nor can it let it go) situation... Having urged a V-termer, he couldn't be seen as being outrun, and he did not expect me to pick up the '*beeda*' (gauntlet) and give him a race.

His goal was to call me out loudly before other juniors, and then berate me at the squadron. Now he had a race on his hands.. Or legs.

So down the slopes we ran, hollering at juniors to get out of the way. It was like a prison yard fight. My lungs got into an overdrive, letting out an other-worldly gasp as I ran like crazy. We covered the distance to the main road, at which point, he called out the X-country captain, and turned me over to him and slowed, holding his waist. He had wisely chosen this a bit out of view of the folks we had just overtaken.

I looked over my shoulder, to see that he had stopped, turning around and was retching his lunch by the roadside. Since my ego problem was with him, I went back to my regular pace, with the cross-country captain none the wiser.. Later that day, at Order fall-in, he glared and muttered 'some Vth termers are not giving it their all'... Our lot guffawed... mentally we said 'No sir, we have not given our utmost, and don't plan to either, till you are there'

The final chapter came another year later, this time, at the Indian Military Academy (IMA). He was the Battalion Under Officer (BUO) of an IMA Battalion, and his Company Jessore, was noted for running the cross country route twice a day, and even at night. He was also participating in the PARA medal competition (rewarded originally from the PARA Commando Battalion of the Indian Army), which had points based on the cross country timing as well.

So we were going through the streets of Kaulagarh village, and I spotted him in the large group. Here, the long downhill of NDA is replaced by a dry, rocky river bed of the Tons river, so again, I was marshalling my breath and running at a manageable pace. The river bed would have Officers timing the run, to better put the best foot forward there, pun intended.

Old memories came to the front. I was running along with a group of my NDA squadron mates - Squadron bonds were still stronger than IMA Company affiliations since we had run together for 2.5 years earlier- and like a pack of *dhores* (Indian wild dogs) coordinating a hunt - we crept up to the now faltering CSM-turned-BUO. This was a bit like the scene in Scarface, where Al Pacino goes hunting for Rebenga in the prison camp. 2-3 of us closed the gap with him.
Do we trip him ? Do we embarrass him for his poor run performance ?

'Looks like we are going to beat the PARA medal types' I shouted excitedly, matching step for step inches from him. I thought we would race past him, and then watch his reaction. But one look at him, and everything changed.
He was out of breath, and missing the steady pace you need to be in for street running. While running that race, one's fitness is usually at a whole new level. After weeks of practice,

road running doesn't even make your breath or heart rate go up, if you have been honestly practicing with the rest of the group for the past few weeks.

The tougher part was ahead, where the round rocks of the dry river bed were to be run on for over a km, but he was faltering well before that. His scores would dip, and he would surely be called out by his officers for being a laggard.

Almost instantly, I and my squadron buddies linked hands in a chain, and lined up behind him. Like a moving, rippling human chain, we gripped his wrist and began taking him along with us in a group, urging him on, so he could make up time. Till the creek bed approached, we got him going, before we let him go, lest anyone get disqualified. By then he had recovered a bit and was in better shape than we found him.

As the race got over, we lay panting in the enclosures. He came over, and said Thanks. After the academy, we would be in separate arms and services, so this was where it all ended. At the squadron social hosted to bid the senior course goodbye, he raved about how our effort helped him get a decent timing in the race. All accounts were squared from cadet days. The grudges were gone that day.

CHAPTER 11 - BEING DEVIOUSLY ENABLED

By the end of the 2nd term, a cadet becomes a Scud missile - not much guidance but speeding at terminal velocity with nary a 'boost coast' and definitely not a 'boost sustain' mode, aimed squarely at making his future terms a bit more comfortable.

By then, One knows 'chappa chappa' (every corner) of the Academy - which corridors of the squadron will have a senior with perpetually broken buttons to mend, and which one would have someone with requests to go to GoI market to fetch satchels of egg rolls and cream puffs. One even becomes devious enough to pick up a few floating 1st termers, to send as bait to squadron offices to see if the Divisional Officers are still there, and if not, then get the day's pristine newspaper.

If they are caught up, and like a grenade, there is some fallout, well, you just tippy toe around the carnage in your Kelachandra shoes - a wildebeest vs crocodile moment in the Okavango delta, played out every day in the Academy.

End of 2nd term was approaching and the tenuous courtship between 5th term sergeants - soon to be appointments - and promising 2nd termers who would fill in their understudy shoes in 3rd term. This being NDA, everything gets abbreviated, so understudies are called 'undies', and so are undergarments, but the usage and its context is key. And barring a squadron where brotherly, forbidden love blooms, this has seriously platonic underpinnings.

Like everything else, understudies are hierarchical, and 2nd termers can spot the gems and lilies and stay clear of sadistic appointments. A few terms back, the Echo Squadron Commander had made the trans-Pune trip from NDA Khadakwasla to the first termers at NDA Wing, and duly managed names of bright sparks, who he made sure got into Echo.

3 years later, long after that officer got posted out, that crop of *'lehlehati'* (swaying) opium was now 6th termers, and being top of their course, both the Academy Cadet Captain (ACC) and the Academy Cadet Adjutant (ACA), were from our squadron, giving us a very close, upfront look as to what their undies did.

So the ACA Undie was like a matador used to seeing dreaded sergeants (bulls) come at the ACA's beckoning in the dead of night in *bajree* order... and God save you from that sergeant's wrath the next day, if he sees you eyeing him during that *in flagrante delicto* like moment.

At the other end of the spectrum, the Divisional Cadet Captains understudies are workhorses getting rogered due to some chronic shortcoming in squadron board decorations, ruefully coated in glitter or some un-Spartan stationary shop stuff as their questionable artistic abilities are stretched to a limit...

My own overstudy was one such pained entity, who was a decent chap, but was always hauled before the DCC or the squadron office... 'No, I won't be a DCC undie for sure', I resolved, as I mouthed gobs of Chyawanprash as my dinner supplement one night.

The sweet spot in all this was - no not the CSM undie, who was seen as the enabler for all that was wrong with the world, but the Squadron Cadet Captain (SCC) undie - who, unlike the CSM's Prime Ministerial workload, was almost Presidential (as in a Parliamentary democracy) in lack of purpose. Getting liberty cards collected and approved for the weekend was his prime purpose.

Yes, that was the sweet spot I should aim for.

So I found myself in this murky pool, when the mournful, soulful Sargeant asked me the question ' Would you want to be my understudy ?' I hemmed and hawed, and in my mind, I thought, 'Well, this guy will end up being a DCC, and I don't fancy being covered in glue and glitter', so I begged off, saying that I had a hard time not getting relegated due to my less than stellar performance in Russian foreign language class, and needed time for that.

His disappointment was palpable, but he went on to choose another coursemate.

But like perestroika and glasnost, change was coming in our world. A brand new 4th battalion was being raised. Which meant that those I considered SCC material , were now exported to this new Battalion, and that would trigger a new wave of appointments.

So the Sergeant who I had spurned, thinking he would be a lowly DCC, now ended up with the top prize of being the SCC. A 1,000 daggers went at my heart, as someone else was now chosen to be his undie. My rage at my own cleverness had left me outsmarted.

That Jan morning, as we stood at Khadkee platform where the NDA Special terminated, a scene befitting Schindler's List selection process unfolded, except in this one, we WANTED to be called out, so that we were chosen to be sent to the new Battalion, where you don't have the legacy of toxic seniors and have a fresh coming-to-America from the wars of Europe like start.

And since the Gods did not shine on me at Khadkee, I was back as a 3rd termer, with no undie-ship in sight.

My lesson learnt was to never let go of opportunities, coz they wont knock twice, and then next knock would be of a forthcoming bathroom session that would soon see you part ways with the extra *bhatura* you imbibed at lunch.

Grab life with everything you got. There are no 2nd chances.

CHAPTER 12 : HANDS-UP MY KHAKI SHORTS

I was in my late teens then ... and have vivid memories of those days as a 19 year old ...
It would happen just before breakfast... I would be standing still .. very still, a blank distant look, waiting for the moment to pass. A man would beckon. Our eyes would meet. In a snap, his hands venturing up my shorts.. grabbing and pulling... hard !
I would wake up sweaty at night. Was it a dream.. ?
Am I unloading a burden I had carried for decades ??

Relax .. this is not a narrative of some dark abuse tale. It takes many hands to raise a kid - and taking that logic a step further, to turn boys into men. And so is the case in a certain 'No Dames Academy'. The hands I refer to are calloused, one-time farmers, who now work as 'cadet orderlies' and are a species unto themselves... So stay tuned before calling the moral police.

How did these wide-pajama'd, Gandhi-topi wearing *taantya* rustics end up with their hands up my shorts ? Like everything else, that's wrong in the sub-continent, The British are to blame.

For the summer heat of India, the khaki shorts were designed for comfort, mobility and with enough pockets to carry pouch loads of ammo, or snacks.

There was a time they were banned in British India, because either the police, or the revolutionaries in Bengal would wear them, as they would aim to fire-bomb/assassinate/sabotage the Raj, riding pillion on a bicycle, wearing, what else but.... khaki shorts.

Being made out of cotton, these would need an immersion in a vat full of starch, and then a heavy iron would give them razor sharp edges and creases. That would give them an extra wide space around the thighs, great for the crown jewels to stay cool so to speak..

When paired with a bush-shirt, with a crisp brass belt buckle holding it all together, it would give the traditional 'brown sahib' look - minus a Sola hat, another product of the British Indian empire.

But how to make 2 starched garments with little 'wriggle room' (no pun intended) to present a uniformed look ? The answer has 2 steps -

1. Tuck the bush shirt into the Khaki Dress shorts (KD shorts), cinched by the drill belt. It would still be billowing out from other portions around the waist... and that's where the waiting army of these orderlies would come in.
2. A cadet would step in front of the orderlies, while they are seated in a row, before breakfast time. Their hands go up the wide-brimmed khaki shorts, yup .. from up the knees , thankfully with enough room for a pair of hands to sneak up.

These mostly sons-of-the-soil Marathi *manoos*, (men) found themselves caught up, in some form of agrarian crisis - and had to leave their tiny plots of land, or were shortchanged out of it by a moneylender, and to make ends meet, took on the 'job at hand' (again, no pun intended), as cadet orderlies.

A quick grab of the bottom of the tucked-in bush shirt, and a hard yank (no, I don't mean a turned-on American)... and the shirt would seamlessly hide neatly into the waist belt.A quick dab of fish oil on your boots, and a wipe down, and you are ready to step into the world, as befitting a cadet.

Does 'accidental contact' happen, as the grabbing and tugging goes on at a rapid pace ..? Well that remains a secret, but mostly traffic flows in their respective lanes.

But these hardy-yet-wily Marathas were the pivot on which your overall comfort within the squadron relied.. From getting bedbug-free furniture for your cabin, having someone get your uniform from the GoI Market, or a paper bag full of egg-rolls and potato *bondas* (fried snack) during study period -they were the folks to rely on when you wanted things done on the 'down low.'

But that's surely not a big deal. Depending on your resourcefulness, and cash tips, better things can happen. Cadets when they become more self aware, start getting ideas ('*par nikalne lagte hain*').. Ideas that get them locking themselves in their cabins during classes, sports, clubs - referred to as locked-in-cabin (LIC) - listening to 'Smooth Criminal' on the cassette player, while cooking a bowl of Maggi noodles or something soul-comforting.

Now, a cash-lubricated nexus with your trusted cadet orderly, will ensure a ready supply of cafeteria *gulab jamuns* on the benign end... and either warn you that an angry Divisional Officer is prowling trying to flush out LIC cadets - and helpfully lock you up in a cabin marked 'furniture'.

During camps, when you are soaking wet, your friendly orderly would show up on the Mess truck, with a 'care package' - dry socks, fresh dungarees, clean and dry innerwear.... the options to ease cadet life are endless.

Same is also said of Mess waiters. As your seniors often lace your food with extra-large salt - lets call that 'table f**king' - or force you to wrap your cutlets and depart for a PT fall-in at 9 PM. a caring mess waiter would pass on a few more bread pieces and cutlets in a napkin as you depart glum-faced.

Years, even decades later, many now high-ranking officers return to the Academy, and seek out their orderlies and Mess waiters, and greet them better than long-lost relatives. Because, if they survived junior term, these unlikely heroes were the reason.

CHAPTER 13 - THE POWER OF THE BAND

One November afternoon, as I went back to NDA, to get my official sealed transcripts to apply for my University of Chicago School of Business (now Chicago-Booth) MBA program, I stepped into the cool haloed portals of the Sudan Block, steps away from the Commandant's office. The large, framed picture of a Gurkha officer with a slight smile triggered a memory, and a name - Cadet Puneet Nath Dutt, who went on to become a Cadet Sergeant Major (CSM) in his 6th term.

CSM Puneet Dutt, was a rare, thinking personality, as opposed to the hard-charging, adrenaline-driven person that usually are called 'Cadet screwing machines' and are chosen for their ability to keep the squadron on its toes - and hence given the privilege to wear the Ashoka emblemed wristband.

Even as a junior, a vast majority of whom are pretty much in shambles under the extreme pressure of 2nd & 3rd term, 'Deadly Dutt', as I would call him in reference to movie star Sanjay Dutt, had a quiet dignity about him, even when he was getting rogered as part of day-to-day life in Echo squadron.

In the hierarchical order of the National Defence Academy (NDA), even the most impetuous, hockey-wielding CSM would be loath to cross paths with the Academy Cadet Adjutant (ACA). While the CSM rules the squadron, the ACA is the king of the Academy, and omnipotent in his domain. The ACA wears shoulder tabs and carries a sword, the CSM wears a wristband with the Ashoka emblem - referred to as a 'band' - and graduates with a rifle, like other 'ordinary' cadets.

But the power of the band is more visceral and fear inducing. While a junior might rarely get to cross paths with the ACA, your life is no more than a sprig of 'hair that grows down south' if you are on the wrong side of the CSM.

In his dress regalia, the ACA takes post at a highly visible spot, usually the Ashoka Pillar crossroads, as he preys on herds of 5th termers, calling them in loaded marching orders with bicycles wrapped around their necks, after lights out.

The CSM operates at the Squadron/Battalion level, and is happy carrying out roasting-toasting of his squadron, and some Battalion juniors to whet his appetite while going to the Mess.

The genesis of this 'transgression' would be found a few weeks earlier. That Autumn term, amidst the slushy mud and the monsoon rain lashing the Sahyadri ranges and Khadakvasla valley where the Academy is situated, Echo squadron won the Cross Country championship, and its trophy - the Glider.

I remember as I and another ex-Echo had driven that weekend from Ahmednagar, where we were doing Young Officers course, and in the tradition of 2/Lts we had seen while ourselves at the Academy, had donned spotless whites with IMA 'Blood and Iron' blazers, and showed up to cheer the Squadron, in person.

Echo squadron does not care about Academics... or tactical acumen in camps... or even Boxing. It only cares about PT - and Cross Country, just like Charlie squadron is about Drill competition, and Alpha is about Football. When we were juniors, much to our misfortune as 2nd termers, the Champion Squadron banner was lost to Golf. .. and all that slide started when Echo was announced 2nd in Cross country, while Golf won the X-country trophy, the 'Glider'.

Oh my... the way back from the cross country venue, the Gliderdrome, was a torment in slow motion. Bataan Death March probably found its encore almost 50 years later. While other squadrons cheered when they were announced in single figures (out of 12), Echo collectively broke into tears, when it was announced 2nd - that too to Golf.

Unsurprisingly, every CSM and cross-country captain promises the moon to the squadron, should Echo win the Glider.

So 2 years after we had seen the Glider go, and 2 years after we had graduated, to see the Glider come to Echo was like the Red Sea parting in 'Ten Commandments'. The 5-6 Ex-Echos who had come there, instantly opened their wallets, and pooled money to buy 'jalebi' and other sweets to take to the Squadron. On the way back, we were literally separated from our motorbikes, and either carried on shoulders, or simply tossed by the mass of delirious juniors.

PN Dutt presided like a king at the CSM's perch at the foot of the squadron stairway. As juniors opened the doors to welcome us, he instantly stepped down, deferred to us, asking us to lead and do 'Echo type' pushups. Even in his moment of glory, he was ready to give space to his erstwhile seniors - like he would when we were 6th termers.

Pushups to the chant of 'Echo .. Echo' were carried out. Another round of photos, bumps and what not..... As we left, he stated the words :

'Mid term mood for squadron..... till mid-term.'

A mid-term mood is granted when a squadron does so well, that the juniors are given relaxation, just like they would when the actual mid-term break happens, usually 3-4 weeks after Cross country, and while the CSM has the prerogative to do whatever he wants INSIDE the squadron, he is on thin ice, when his lets his squadron enjoy mid-term in the Academy proper.

It means, even juniors can simply go to the Mess without being rogered in the way, or can walk back from movies, without awaiting torment by sergeants en route - and that's the prerogative of the ACA.

Reports then emerged, that his proclaiming mid-term mood was called out by his fellow-coursemate, the ACA. Things came to a head, when after a movie screening, when the ACA wanted the cadets to stay back, CSM Dutt got his squadron to stand up and walk out, much to the fury of the ACA, whose authority was disregarded, as Echo squadron walked by merrily out of the Auditorium.

So, in all probability, CSM Dutt must be letting the Squadron enjoy what he had promised, and he would stand up for them. For sure, he would know that the ACAs hackles would be raised, as his squadron decamped en masse, but what he had promised, he would back it up.

It probably got escalated to the Adjutant, where Dutt stood his ground, and prevailed

His habit of standing up in defence of his juniors and troops, probably was with him, till he breathed his last, fighting terrorists in Kashmir, and getting the highest peacetime gallantry award - the Ashok Chakra in the process.

We never met after that fateful cross country day in 1994.

After that visit , I visited the Squadron in 2008. There, at the CSM's perch, was the 'Replica' - an identical brass copy of the Glider that is given when a squadron wins the cross-country thrice.One of those wins was under Dutt's watch. I stood admiring the metal aircraft for a minute or two, thinking about the collective sweat and occasional blood that went into securing it, for eternity.

Batches of cadets will come and go, but the Replica will stay embedded there .... for good, just like PN Dutt's portrait in the haloed chambers of the Sudan Block... also for good.

But CSM Dutt was destined for eternal glory. Less than 2 years after commissioning, on a July day in 1997, he surrounded a party of foreign (read Pak/Afghan/Chechen) militants, in downtown Srinagar. He shot one militant at point blank range, then led his men into combat with the entrenched militants, ultimately sacrificing his life.

He led his men as a cadet, he continued to do so as a warrior. RIP 'Deadly' Dutt.

CHAPTER 14 - PAY PARADE PANGS

Back in the 90s, the closest a 2/Lt comes into some serious amount of cash - in the 1st year or service - is when he is unfortunate to be detailed with drawing the pay of the troops from the local bank, on the 1st of the month.

100 Rs notes being the highest denomination, a huge steel trunk - the kind where family photo albums go to rest amidst mothballs till eternity - was required to bring in the moolah to the unit. And one day, it was my turn to do the job.

Capt Sanjay (RIP), would always have a twinkle in his eye, whether he is pulling you up for not landing the basketball from the other end of the court, or summoning you to visit the local ammunition dump at 2 AM in Punjab winters, on a guard check, leaned back in his chair, polished boots on the table as he drawled.

'God save you if even a single rupee is missing' as I nervously checked and rechecked my standard, Officer-issued 9 mm Beretta pistol strapped in a holster. I could not make out if he was advising me out of concern, or well nigh wishing for some notes to come up short, on their own. I believe it was reluctant advice, as I was under his care, and any shortcomings on my account would be seen as his too, hence the need for everything to go properly.

This being 1994, with Punjab still in the grip of a waning militancy, a convoy with escort roared out of the barbed wire enclosure - , a recce troop Jonga, Light-Machine-gun manning trooper up top,, a 1-tonner Nissan vehicle bearing the cash chest, and another Jonga carrying armed-to-the-teeth soldiers bringing up the rear, engines running, tailboards down, awaited my arrival.

Very effortlessly, these tank men had switched to an anti-insurgency mode, complete with a 'casually lethal' look never seen when they are usually slathering on large splotches of axle grease on their black dungarees ... Now, heels barely an inch above the ground, they piled on the open-tarpaulin truck, fingers on the ready on a mix of weaponry that included carbines, and AKs, the latter probably once belonging to a slain militant.

So while on most months, the local bank was a short jog away, on the day I was to draw pay, I was told by the local manager that we could either wait for the pay to show up God-knows-when, or make our way to Patiala 30 km away, and pick it from the main branch itself.

With no cellphones, we got the radio man to let the Adjutant know of the situation, and were promptly told to 'Not return without pay', and be back by 1 PM' - leaving the finer details to figure it out to me, as the call went dead.

Calling back is usually not a good idea, even in the best of times.

So off we went to Patiala, in the heat that only paddy-growing Punjab can muster in its stillness and humidity, the 3 vehicle convoy given a wide berth even by the maniacal

Roadways bus drivers. Cash was collected, counted, and recounted, as we worked through the heat, well past 1 PM.

As we headed back, the Senior JCO accompanying me whispered 'saab ji, pukh lagee ae mundyaa nu ' (the boys are hungry) in my ears. The lead Jonga driver had cleverly taken a turn before the cantonment entrance, and right on the way past some of the crispest, deep brown *cholley-samosas* served with white radish shavings on top and a pat of fast melting butter, with elephant ear size *bhatooras* one gets only in Punjab.

For sure, their own official meal was 10 min away, but since gullible Lieutenants have dangling heartstrings just waiting to be pulled, I gestured the convoy to a halt, and we dismounted, and soon, 6-8 fierce men were stuffing their faces into hot *bhaturas*, sponsored by yours truly.

What I was not aware of was that the pay parade had also assembled in the Regiment, and we REALLY needed to be there on time - with cash. So after another 90 minutes, we rolled into the unit - the word of us snacking had already reached the unit, thanks to the eagle-eyed sentries at the nearby checkpoint, who had radioed back, while the entire unit stood assembled under the midday sun, waiting for pay - as Capt Sanjay paced, red-faced and agitated.

The sight of Capt Sanjay pacing at the Regimental HQ was enough to mess up my aftertaste.

'Where the Hell were you... ! and how could you eat before reporting back ?', flicking an odd crumb from my tunic. I was deeply embarrassed, at this cock-up of a basic task, despite my best intentions.

10 min later, he re-emerged, directed me to take the pay to the unit lines ASAP, and make haste pronto to the Officers Mess, as some hell was breaking loose there, while preparing for that evening's party.

That evening, after trying to evade him unsuccessfully, he gestured to me to sit down. He already knew what had happened, and told me, almost in a paternal manner.

'Relax, I know you meant well ... but you are in charge. So YOU control the entire activity. Take feedback, but this is not a democracy, so you need to exert your judgement and maintain control, else the boys will take you for granted.'

I did many pay parades after that, and tasks of increasing complexity, involving coordination and troop control, but while being receptive to feedback, I always went in with a plan in my head, and that would include a meal break, but after the pay had been dispersed and the task over.

Even in today's era of automated pay transfers, the pay parade is held to ensure the junior officers get to know the men they will eventually lead in combat. The money aspect is only incidental in the scheme of things.

CHAPTER 15 : MAIN BHI SALMAN KHAN ('I am also a Bollywood Hero')

".. and lastly, there will be no shooting, hunting of any form, whatsoever, in the exercise area.', came the clipped, slightly metallic voice over the Regimental radio net, as me and my subaltern, a Lt, shot knowing glances within the lean-to.

For a tank crew, a lean-to is a shelter from heaven, wherein the barrel of the main gun is depressed (brought down, there is nothing 'mentally wrong' with it), and a tent tarpaulin is draped over it, and then raised again, forming a quick-to-setup tent that will hold in the strongest of winds.

The CO had rushed back to the unit location in Punjab, with the 2 I/C, while the regiment had deployed over a 5 km frontage in the Bikaner-Lunkaransar area, in the deserts of Rajasthan, where time crawls slowly, and the desert flies breed prolifically. One of the Squadron commanders was now in-charge, one with a penchant for roasted meat, now and then.

And considering the source of the orders, our skepticism was '*jaayaz*' (valid). The officiating Squadron Commander now relaying orders had just been liberated from Staff College preparation purgatory, and was a formidable shooter, with a cross-attachment with the National Security Guards (NSG) turning his 'cavalier' aim into a 1-inch group of bullets on a target, after spending a year firing German Heckler & Kochs and MP-5s on silhouetted foreheads.

We lived in interesting times - Salman Khan, the chocolate boy from marriage videos that turned into movies, where families went to scout the latest wedding trousseaus, and hubbies went to sleep in the air conditioned cinemas, had just been apprehended by the local nature-loving community of Bishnois, who fiercely, often violently, resisted any hunting, chopping of trees or any trespass in the natural domain the desert offers.

But then, there is only so much watery '*moong dal*' you can have, without a regular supply of fresh veggies. So around Day 12 of such a state of meals, a .22 rifle was smuggled out of a crew man's bedding holdall - the one he would never unroll till now, for some reason.

With the senior officers gone, or too far away to supervise, the young Captains were now marauding like *nilgais*, (Indian blue bull), and had their trusted, chosen men on guard duty - at the motor pool, on the approach road, forming a close circle of trust on duty that evening, all very hush-hush.

The .22 was meant to dispatch any *teetar* (black partridges) but the hope was to bag a small deer species called 'chinkara'. We wanted no deal with its more famous cousin, the Black Buck, which got Salman in hot water, and behind cold steel bars.

The Officers Mess's top cook, Murthy had been requisitioned, by the stroke of a pen, to our Squadron, on the innocuous reason that 'after all, non-combatants should also experience exercise area rigors like frontline tankmen'.

The 2IC nodded along approvingly, at this new found care amongst his young officers for the 'langar parade', and signed him off to our clutches.... um care.

The Technical Adjutant did his part, by keeping the best 4x4 Jonga of the recce (reconnaissance) troop, duly shown as 'out of order', and jacked up on a pile of bricks, with the tires removed. These all terrain vehicles had specially souped up engines, so they could go at blazing speed in the sandy deserts, ahead of the main tank columns, and often deep in enemy territory.

The Brigade HQ had a nasty habit of sending the Brigade Supply and Transport Officer aka BSTO (an overweight major jokingly called 'Busto' as he had a proper bustline), and he would commandeer the best jeeps/Jongas from units of the Brigade. This we had learnt the hard way ..

Not any more sir, as this is the desert, and we will protect our secrets (and Jongas) !

We were supposed to be watched over by the jittery CO of the adjacent Mechanised Infantry battalion next to us, but as our wise Motor Transport Officer (MTO) drawled in a fake Texan accent over some hot chai - he was too caught up to impress the Brigade Commander given this was his first exercise as part of the Armoured Brigade, so as Thakur from Sholay would say 'Garam hai loha... kar do chot' (Strike, as the iron is hot).

Luck permitting, and if all our shots lined up, the same heat was expected to rise from the mess kitchen, as in the concluding scene of every Asterix comic - albeit catching a boar in cream sauce was rare - but it's Indian cousin - malai deer qorma might land down our wide open gullets, IF the timing and shooting was right.

Just like our infantry compatriots, the moon was kept a tab of. It needed to rise late, so we could set out in complete darkness, but cast enough of a glow, so we didn't land head first into the 1000s of unmarked wells that dotted the landscape. These wells had been dug over many years, but then in the 80s, the Indira Gandhi canal brought pristine Himalayan waters to the desert, rendering these brackish wells useless - and open and unmarked for any jeep or tank to fall in at night.

As soon as the evening 'stand-to' (a drill meant to have troops in position form the night watch) was observed, a flurry of activity took form.

Tarpaulins were ripped open, hidden jeep wheels were magically produced and attached to bare axles, and large yellow floodlights were mounted to the rooftop bars. All in a matter of minutes.

The camouflage nets of a T-72 tank served as the overhanging cushion on which low-value 2nd Lieutenants such as myself could be tethered, more to provide ballast for the bouncy jeep - but more importantly, to mask any shikaar (hunting kills) we had that day by hoisting our skinny butts atop the tarp hiding the carcass.

Come sundown, we set off in the still shimmering desert, away from the deployed area, and into the *keekar* scrub. The quiet .22 rifle was now accompanied by a regular 7.62 mm Self loading rifle, ideal for dispatching the local 'chinkara' deer, and also repelling any obnoxious wild boars, who would otherwise not be deterred by a .22 bullet. A gore injury from a wild boar tusk would be a bit inconvenient to explain to the pretty lady Regimental Medical Officer (RMO) in the morning, so best avoided.

In an hour or so, a suitable sized *chinkara* was found, and dispatched by a well aimed shot, although we were barely a km from a Bishnoi village, that we had to flank on the way back. In our meticulous planning, the way out was different from the way in, as any self-respecting patrol is taught to do, but it is hard to mask the sound of a Jonga groaning in the desert sand with a bunch of men hanging off camo netting, casting yellow strobes of light in the darkness.

'Who is this .. identify yourself', came the sound over the now-silent radio set, and we froze. The clipped accent of the Brigade commander came over the airwaves, and about a km to our left, the rotating red light atop his Gypsy could be seen moving in double time, towards us. Our driver was frozen till our Quartermaster, a Captain, hoisted him out of his seat, and slid in as he gunned the jeep.

The only saving grace for us was that the desert trail was over dozens of sand dunes, so he could only spot us only when we hit the very top of the '*dhora*' (sand hill).

'Stop you bloody fools', along with ear-reddening abuses in chaste Punjabi came in a torrent over the radio, as we saw his Gypsy aiming straight for us. In desperation, we turned the headlights and the flood lights off - driving the jeep in almost pitch darkness, aimed nowhere in particular in the desert. To go back to the unit lines, or its general direction even would be suicidal, and there will be plenty of time to astro-navigate, our way back using the stars- if we got out of this by some miracle.

But we still had the carcass of the deer under the camouflage netting, with me sitting on top of it.

'Youngster , be ready to ditch it' ... (I had not been called by my name in months, being a green 'youngster')

'Ditch what sir ?'

'The damn *chinkara*, you moron ! '.

So all this would come to nothing... The poor chinkara died unappreciated, as I fiddled with the netting, trying to pull its now-tangled head from the nets.

Our eyes met, his eyes glazed in death, and mine in terror, as I prepared to roll it off the jeep.

At the last moment, just as I was saying a silent prayer in my head, we stopped abruptly.There was silence punctuated by the chirping of 100s of crickets and denizens of the desert. Hundreds of fireflies moved about, backlit by 1000s of stars. We went about a minute's drive away from the jeep track, helpfully hidden by a fine sand storm dust.

Time ticked by.

'Let's move back' said my subaltern..

'Not now' grunted a wizened Captain, fresh from a tenure from counter-insurgency operations... and rightly so.

Within seconds, the Commanders Gypsy came screaming down the sand hill, gunning past us hiding 300 m or so away. Had we started a minute back, he would have almost run into us. Chaste swear words kept coming over the radio set. We felt like the German U-571 sitting on the ocean floor, while depth charges rained on top of her.

15 min later, we gingerly made our move, slinking back into the unit area, headlights off. Dinner prep did not begin till after midnight, as we were worried about a visit, but capable guards with flashlights deployed towards the Brigade HQ location served to avoid any surprises, and signal us if needed.

For a day, I was the proud owner of the head of the chinkara, which I thought I would have a taxidermist mount, but in the morning, one of the Captains told me to 'get rid of it', and off it went in the desert sands.

That was as close to being a Bollywood movie star that I ever wanted to be in this life.

CHAPTER 16 : ON TENACITY

Tenacity is one thing one graduates with, in spades, after 3 years of blood, sweat and occasional tears at the NDA. Be it clearing large mounds of dug up soil on your own, for days for a garden, one scoop at a time, or plodding through never ending meetings and emails, one tends to put the proverbial one foot before the other and literally soldiers on. Heaven may or may not have the riches of King Nero, but for sure there would be a Roman trooper shivering in the cold doing guard duty at the eternal palace.

So today, we find course mates who could not wear their anklets correctly during their Drill Square Tests, now commanding entire formations as Major-Generals. Cousermate humor , a few years back was if the Pakistanis want to take Siachen, that would have been the ideal time, for them to make their move, as all 3 infantry battalions deployed up there were manned by people who, at the Academy, would be loath to man their Sergeant's posts, earning the sobriquet 'eating toast, not taking post' amongst fellow never-do-gooders.

Of course, professionally, they were second to none, but coursemates take no notice of whatever stellar career progression their buddies might have had. For us, the same Brigadier was a toast-hogging sergeant from decades back.

Non-swimmers, who would sink at the 3-foot mark in the pools, spewing out that Tuesday's *Chola-bhatoora* lunch – went on to become lake swimmers in the vast Khadakwasla lake... just by virtue of tenacity.

And what better (or worse, depending on viewpoint), a place to unearth one's own depth or shallowness in this department, than at the modern day Colosseum – the Gliderdrome, where the 8.2 km cross country run originates and ends, as about 2,000 cadets scamper across, unmindful of its barbed wire fence, the thistles clinging to one's Kelachandra shoes (yes.. it's a brand, and a v durable one). Similar to a mule in disposition, a Kelachandra shoe lasts through the thick black Maharashtrian clay, long after the Nike/Puma/Power shoes have been swallowed up.

In the running department, the Maharashtrian cadets prove formidable. Surnames like Adhaw, Valimbe, Kakade dominate the medal tally as they run in conditions they have grown up in, and with a light frame, are much more fleet footed and light breathing than the aloo-paratha stuffing North Indians like myself. One of such cadets – lets call him Cadet 'Joy' – was an acute shammer, sleepy-eyed and constantly dozing, but could run like a horse, when unleashed. We were pleasantly surprised in junior terms when he won one of the 10 or 12 medals given out, thereby marking his future tenure as someone who would be left alone, given his medal win as a junior.

Come our 5th term, just one term short of graduation, and our hopes of earning a hard-earned rest, were shattered by the appointment of a tough-as-nails, Academy Cadet Adjutant, let's call him 'Birju'. Unlike the more urbane Naval cadet who ended up his counterpart as Academy Cadet Captain, Birju had been a bane of those of us who had to cross his post to get to the Mess, all through the last 6 months, when he was a Sergeant.

'Dammit ... lovely Dammit' was his calling card, and it does sound like an oxymoron, but that's what he would grunt when he would have a bunch of us lifting our bicycles over our head... and Birju was a v capable runner.

So, when the race got over that hot March afternoon, we were surprised to learn that Cadet Joy had not been on the medal podium. And how close he was, reflects the tenacity that kicked in that morning - from someone already set as the best in his lot.

Birju had been in the front runners of a pack with the best runners of the 6 terms of the academy. His medal was not only expected, but assured. Somewhere, in the last km, around where the turn from the Equitation Lines to the Glider dome is, he began experiencing cramps. The photos taken by the Academy photographers – Goel studios uncover a story of grit.

Like a British Spitfire limping across the channel after enduring a strafing from a Luftwaffe Messerschmidt 109, Birju kept running clutching his abdomen, and in intense pain, that only runners know. Determined not to lose his medal spot, yet he felt himself falling behind, till the final turn, where one can see the 'enclosure' (space that closes at 2-min intervals) one would land in. Since the end enclosure is visible from about 800 m away, after the 1st enclosure, one is sure to miss an enclosure before their own eyes, so the seniors told us.

So in the last 200 m, as the rope guideways narrowed, and the first 9 cadets, assured medals, sailed through, the spot for the last medal was now a 2-man race between Joy and Birju. A set of 3 photos captured the moment. In the first one, a grimacing Birju is a couple of steps behind Joy, who looks self-assured and confident of the final medal spot. The medals are given out based on a slip of paper a runner has to take from a staffer, so as to make sure the order is correct.

In the second picture, just as Joy's hand is out – like a relay runner picking up the baton – Birju is seen aiming for the space between the slip-issuer and Joy. In a flash, like a hawk diving in on a careless student's lunch sandwich during recess - he plucks the slip from the NCO issuing it, leaving Joy bewildered. They would then run at their top speed, but Birju's hold on the slip, and the lead of 1 step would be too much to surmount. The harder Joy ran those final steps, the more determined Birju seemed to be to maintain his hold and lead. Once in the enclosure, he collapsed, dry-heaving and retching, but with the slip still in his hand. Joy sat as if his world had collapsed around him. He would regain the medal as a 6th termer, but at that moment, he was dumbstruck.

Both went on to do spectacularly well in their chosen fields – Birju as a tankman, and Joy as a pilot, so am sure, on some desert or mountain landscape, they would still continue to display tenacity, and set an example – as the situation arose.

In life, there is always someone hungrier than you who would try to snatch that medal from your hands.

CHAPTER 17 : EARTY WITTICISMS

Hilarity and wit rise like a cloud of heated steam from a red hot 'dosa' *tava* (flat pan) sprinkled with water droplets, when the mostly rural soldiery meets and interacts with the mostly city raised Central/Army/Public school educated young officer corps, inducted as 2nd Lieutenant (now that intake happens as a Lieutenant). Nowadays, we do see a welcome shift in intake to a more non-metro and rural and JCO/NCO family kids joining as officers, but the Romanized (Hindi written in English script) discourses between the 2 can be a minefield to traverse.

Many of these have already entered immortal territory in various Officer Mess anecdotes - such as '*Saab, mera 'family' beemar hai*' (Sir, My family is sick) - with the key difference in usage being that when a soldier uses the term 'family' it refers ONLY to the wife, not the entire 'family')... but it can be very concerning when heard for the first time.

While studying for my pre-course, (a course taught within the unit, before the actual course), I was put under the charge of a mournful Dogra '*daffadar*' (a three-striped sergeant') Dharam Singh Pathania, shortened to 'Dharma' in the Sikh-Dogra unit I was in.His claim to fame was not basketball, or shooting or even cooking a great daal fry in the desert - Dharma would specialise in sending greenhorn 2/Lts to Young Officers (YO) Courses with a solid pre-course training.

Dharma even sported a Military Police style leather-and-brass Armband, with TDM (Training Daffadar Major) in shining brass letters, and was even allowed to carry his own cane. His grandeur was of course, frowned upon by the JCOs and the 'Woordie Major' but Dharma was rumored to be capable enough to march up to the CO's office and give his view on something he felt worthy of the Old Man knowing, in matters pertaining to training in the unit.

Sitting in a Pre course 1-person class, meant that one could sneak a glance at own coursemates' slogging in the hockey fields or running around for some inspection readiness - doing anything but study for their own Infantry/Mechanised YO courses, while I would be sitting in the garage, with a blackboard in front of me, and a 10:30 AM date with 'A' Squadron langar's famed *pakoras* - much before pakoras became a vehicle of mass economic upliftment in certain circles.

Any eye contact, with such course mates, was best avoided, although not after a wide-mouth snap of the *pyaaz* (onion) pakora at hand.

'*Laksh, lagaawat, aam bayaan - Ho sakey to diagram*' translates into very sound advice- while called to explain the functioning of a T-72's hydro-cyclonic filter, just stating the purpose, location and general description - and IF possible, a diagram, would be considered enough effort, for a 5 mark question.

An 'AC Denko' fuel pump would have a 'kampan setter' in it for drawing in fuel. After much head-scratching, including a hesitant query to the Technical Adjutant - it took an assorted array of Capts and Lts to figure out that 'compensator' was the term being referred to.

The advice would often transcend into more benign strategies.

'Nagar ki ERE, apni apni jawaabdaari ' was another pithy earthy expression used. ERE - extra-regimental employment, refers to deputations, and postings -where, unlike the protective embrace of the unit, on these EREs, one is supposed to be without a safety net - and basically be responsible for own actions amidst others from different units, and work culture.Wise gyaan indeed.

Soon after learning just as much from an actual Corps level exercise, it was time to bid adieu to the blazing plains of Punjab, and go to monsoon-drenched Ahmednagar for 6 months of 'relief' and spicy samosas delivered right within the Lecture Hall.

The Brigade Major (BM) - himself a product of a 1857-era Horse unit, came up to the T-72 cut model (a tank with outer turret removed, to show the interiors for trainings) sized me up and said, ' If I blindfold you, and ask you to identify 10 components by touch, can you do that ?'

This is actually a great way to know your tank, in case one is in a desert night, and there has been an electrical outage within the tank that now has zero visibility inside. and I thanked my stars for those late April nights sitting in the Binjrasar desert sand, on my tank during Exercise Bhawani Khadka, with just Daffadar Dharma, going over various tank components, and my ability to locate them.

Would I embarrass myself ? Or worse, let down my unit ? What would Dharma say ?

I paused, looked at Dharma.. who nodded v subtly. And so it began - from the easier 'air bottle valves' (for air starting the tank with compressed air - a feature now gone), to 'pre-set band selector toggle switch' (on the radio set), to the more hairy breech block locking pins (which are heavily grease smeared, and can only be felt by fingers) of the 125 mm main gun... when it came to locating the bilge pumps, or the turret traverse electromagnet and hydro cyclonic filter, I was already anticipating and moving the next question that the BM would ask..

'Good job' muttered the Brigade Major, his chance of putting a youngster a few notches down now gone. Dharma smiled the briefest of smiles. Word then got to the CO - right down to the questions I was asked and responded.

In July, when our batch assembled at the School of Armoured Warfare, in distant Ahmed Nagar, at commencement of the course, the question came from the 'Chief Instructor' - So who all have had pre-course training ?, as he looked around at shoulder insignias of Officers from regiments renowned for their training programs.

Just as Dharma had warned me to , I remained quiet - and so did a bunch of those who actually did go through similar programs. Most of them would be from v traditional, British Indian Army heritage units, with pre-course gyaan distilled, and passed by word-of-mouth, from one generation of NCOs, to another of Young Officers.

After all, we are in it to compete ... and for sure 'Nagar ki ERE.. apni apni jawabdari' was on full display, from Day ONE.

CHAPTER 18 : ENDURANCE HIKE TO Pt. 4311

Bollywood movie 'Kondhana' - about the capture of a hilltop fortress bearing the same name - ruled the roost at Box offices some years back, joining the '100 crore Rupee' club in less than a week. The storyline revolves around the capture of said fort in late 1600s -ruled by Mughals under Emperor Aurangzeb, who had shrewdly deputed a brave Hindu Rajput 'qiledaar' (garrison keeper), named Rathore (played by another real life royalty scion, Saif Ali Khan). It was rumored, at that time, to be impregnable, with garrison of Turkish and Kurdish soldiers standing guard.

As forts go, Kondhana was indeed nearly impregnable in the late 1600s. Built on top of a forested volcanic plateau, it had very steep approaches, thereby eliminating the need for tall fort ramparts, like in the traditional forts. Surrounded by the 3-month long monsoon clouds in the rainy season, with thick forests crawling with snakes, bears and tigers and ready-to-fight tribals known as 'Mavalis' , in a location that was remote, rugged and inhospitable.

The fort was wrested - by Tanaji Malsure, a brave commander of Maratha ruler Shivaji, who perished in its capture. Sensing no easy way to breach the fort's perimeter, he threw a monitor lizard '*ghorpad*' with a rope around its waist up the fortress wall. After a few failed attempts, Tanaji was reported to have given a last warning to the lizard, failing which, she would meet the business end of a sword, after which, the lizard, held to the wall, and the guerilla warriors clambered up, fastened additional ropes down the ramparts, and gained enough numbers to fight hand-to-hand combat, and win the fort for Shivaji.

The tenacious monitor lizard was found to have perished, but still maintaining its iron grip on the stone rampart of the fort.Empire building has been the bane of many rulers across history, and Aurangzeb, who sat on the all-powerful Mughal throne at Agra fort, could not resist succumbing to the same impulses as Alexander... or present day rulers.

When India's 'West Point' - the National Defence Academy - was set up in the shadow of the same fort, its' historical significance would have 'consequences' on the sweat-soaked lives of cadets. For starters, the very first camp, aptly named 'Camp Greenhorn' is spent either in the sticky rain-soaked mud during the Fall term, or in the baking hot dust when it dries out in summer - causing equal measures of misery irrespective of the time of year one went.

In line with the military's reliance on cartography, the name Kondhana... or Singhgarh (name given by Emperor Shivaji upon winning the fort) - is referred to as 'Point 4311' the number referring to the height in feet of the fort from sea level.

A 22 km round trip from NDA flanking a vast reservoir, would be called 'Endurance Hike to Pt 4311' in Academy lingo. By laying out the route along a vast reservoir, there is no scope of taking any shortcuts, which if caught, would result in the award of even more 'Endurance Hikes' (EH) thus completing a vicious cycle of Crime and Punishment. Denizens of this select club of EH awardees could be considered as present-day equivalent of penal convicts being sent to Australian settlements from Victorian England.

Every Sunday, at 6:30 AM, cadets wearing Olive green dungarees, and wearing a carrying a 'Scale B' - comprising a battle gear outfit devised in WWII Burma - with a blanket, mosquito net and raincoat - irrespective of weather, and also including over 20-plus items chosen for their potential to cause distress by their absence - a snakebite kit, with a rusty blade that would be more toxic than any snake bite, a 'housewife kit' with sewing kit, toothbrush, toothpaste, PT shoes and your packed lunch and water bottle.

You could well run the Endurance Hike, but if you are not able to produce a toothbrush, or some silly item, then the hike is 'Not counted' (NC) - a shock that had many grown up 19 year old cadets cry in sheer agony at the prospect of repeating the run on the next Sunday.

The chief tormentor in our days was *Subedar* (Junior Commissioned Officer) Rajan - a 6 foot tall, dark Guardsman from Tamil Nadu, who would refer to himself , in 3rd person, as a *'kaala bhooth'* (Dark Ghost). Since he was a Services level Basketball player, promotions came fast to him, and that caused some consternation to other JCOs who had tenures in Kashmir valley, or Siachen glacier.

They would insinuate Rajan as a 'Sports Quota' type, and probably that triggered his fastidious urge to screen hapless cadets with a fine comb (which was also a part of the items one was supposed to carry). It would be as if Doctor Mengele himself had come to preside over the demise over your Endurance Hike completion prospects.

These hikes would come and go as per the Commandants of the Academy - An Army general would reinstate them as the 'Academy seemed to be going soft', while a Navy/Air Force Commandant would remove them - to provide a human touch. Not surprisingly, during my tenure these were handed out like free candy.Over time, the edge of the paved road would have a metallic gleam - lined with flakes of metal from the studded boots we wore, up and down the fort.

But going on these hikes had a certain 'stud value'. Irrespective of your term, you would be allowed to rest that Sunday, provided you completed it, of course. In some 'hot' squadrons, going on these punishments was still considered preferable to facing the torment that went on inside the squadron.

During rainy weather, when most college teenagers would gingerly climb up the mountain in their Nike/Adidas lightweight shoes, you would be sprinting up in your loaded packs, and heavy boots, yelling 'Move to a side, you clods !' to those lily-livered civilians, as the simpering damsels would ooh and aah, or berate their boyfriends for not being so 'fast and agile', - compliments heard about later when taking same damsels' single girl friends out for a date, when on Liberty to Pune'.

On returning back, the most intrepid would shower, change, and get our Liberty passes to Pune signed - where a massive burger, called 'King Burger' of indeterminate bovine meat - awaited us at a reasonable price point.

But doing Endurance Hikes in the 4.5 hours, gave you a level of fitness that would be elusive later in your life.

Ah.. the days !

CHAPTER 19. C-A-W-N-P-O-R-E

The British Raj depicted in Ivory Merchant movies ('Far Pavilions' et al), comes with oodles of nostalgia draped in Sola hats and evenings under the tropical night skies lit with fireflies is enough to make anyone swoon over it. It came packaged with references to 'frangipani', 'memsahibs' and other balderdash, till those who retired off to a countryside cottage on a nice pension croaked off to the 'eternal Raj in the Sky'. In those gatherings, the name 'Cawnpore' drew abhorrence, symbolising the treacherousness of the 'sepoys' towards their British officers and families during that hot summer of 1957.

It has now come to light that just like the 'Black Hole of Calcutta' and the Bengal Famine of 1942, there was a behind-the-scenes British component to it with exaggerations and half-truths to render a volatile atmosphere more combustible.

When the 'Great Indian Mutiny/First War of Indian Independence (depending on whether you see it from British or Indian eyes) of 1857 broke out, the British were taken by surprise. Pre-1857, despite the introduction of beef/pork tallow laden greased cartridges - meats considered verboten for Hindu and Muslim troops, quite a few British officials had taken on a genuine desire to learn more about the ancient Indian culture and lifestyles - smoking *hookahs* was commoner than the sight of a present-day hookah bar, and many East India Company officials spoke fluent '*Hindoostani*', and had Indian spouses/'partners'.

Colonials of that pre-1857 era had officers such as David Ochterlony, and Major Skinner (of Skinner's Horse fame, presently 1 HORSE of Indian armoured units), , who genuinely took to learning more about this recently colonised land and its people. So great was their interest in India and her people that they were mocked by their own British compatriots as 'Loony Akhtar' for their deep-seated desire to be a part of the people they were coming to rule over.

As with any attack, with the element of surprise with it, the flames of Mutiny charged across the parched plains and kingdoms of northern India, across regions of Bengal, United Provinces, all the way to Delhi and further west.. At one such place, Cawnpore, after a particularly long series of sieges, and bloody skirmishes, a truce was called to let the British women, children and wounded out, and board boats on the Ganges river to take them away from the conflict zone.

While this lot was boarding, from a riverside '*ghat*', Satichaura Ghat - a gunshot - fired from unidentified source pedigree rang out - leading to another fusillade, and the ghastly spectacle of a massacre of all Britishers - men, women and children. Till date, no one knows who fired it - the rebels or the British in panic, but soon bodies were bobbing on the Ganges - and the spot was named 'Massacre Ghat' for obvious reasons.

Of course, when the tide turned in early 1858, the British sought vengeance and dispatched captured Indian rebels, at the same ghat- just like ISIS did with Iraqis at one of Saddam's palaces overlooking the Tigris. In fact 'Cawnpore' became a rallying cry similar to Coventry and Dunkirk, 90 years later, during WWII, as they retook India the next year.

I am inclined to believe that this was no sporadic incident - it was more like 'burning bridges' and the Rebel leaders shed British non-combatant blood, to ensure there was no going back, for the fact would be that from that point on, the British will take (and did take) a 'no prisoner' policy).

Nearby Lucknow, and its British Residency too came under siege, till a relief force marched up from Bengal, and Generals Neil and Havelock hung, or put to sword countless Indian peasants along the Grand Trunk Road, akin to the Romans crucifying early Christians along the Appian Way.

Cut to 2007, and I find myself in London on a business trip, and decide to take a tour of the Tower of London. Just like the famed ravens strutting about, there were the 'Beefeater' wardens, and one particular old peacock who seemed a bit flush in the cheek, ruddy in color and reeky in breath.

While we waited for the tour to begin, he began querying in a gruff voice, where the visitors hailed from. He was pretty solicitous of the Americans 'Ah Springfield ! very nice' .. sneering towards the Germans (mimicking goose-steps), and contemptuous towards the French (blowing raspberries).

Soon he espied some fellow brown-skinned Indian exotics. 'Ah Delheeeee' he sneered, when he heard the reply from an Indian couple, in a tone octet higher, with none of the amusement. His gaze fell on me and without the 'sir', he called out 'you.. where are you from', as he began turning his back without waiting for my reply.

'C-A-W-N-P-O-R-E' came my drawn-out reply, to which he froze just like 'Papa Kulikov' does when hit mid-stride by Major Koenig's sniper shot in 'Enemy at the Gates'. While I am from Banaras, (Varanasi), it's on the same Ganges, yet within the same state.

Sensing his tone, I had to come with a riposte, and Cawnpore would be a name that would wind him up a bit.

Most non-British visitors could not discern what it was about.. but amongst the Indians in the crowd, a wave of laughter rippled through. He turned, no longer jovial, and then 'Hrrrummphed' his way further.

The warm glow through the cockles of my heart stayed with me through the rest of the day.

CHAPTER 20 - CANNED RESPONSES

On a much smaller scale than the CO's *durbaar* (all hands parade), there is another mini-*darbaar*, that holds equal, if not more potential of landing a fresh-from-Academy 2/Lt in harm's way. This one is the Senior-Subaltern's gathering, usually in the Mess, around 1900h, between the bewitching hour when you return from squash or any other officer-like game, and turn up at Mess, at the designated hour, having duly inspected and sampled the very first of appetisers of the evening.

Discretion is the better part of valor, and like observant hyenas watching year-old deer straggle along their fearsome pack at the watering hole, you know better than reaching your paw out, and coming in between a fresh cheese-bread-*pakora* that's the focus of a Major-saab's eye.

Our indulgent Mess NCO, Moorthy, would have kept a plate aside for the youngsters, which we would dip into, under pretext of checking in the kitchen.Many were the attempts made to poach Moorthy, to attach him to the Brigade Mess or elsewhere, or try to send him 'on special request' at events in far-off Chandigarh, but our 2 I/C swatted away such attempts with the contempt they deserved.

We averted a mini-disaster, when the Commander's wife's handwritten menu card came back with a soup called 'Gazpacho Andalous', which unknown to me, was a Spanish Cold soup. This was a double whammy for me, as I did not even know that cold soups existed, and that they had made their way into an Indian Army gathering.

Moorthy was smart enough to figure out what it was, based on the prodigious amount of ice ordered for a Sunday brunch, that too from a specific shop near Patiala's 22-number *faatak* (railroad crossing).

'This ice is for the soup, and not for the drinks' he muttered as he unloaded it first, prying it away from the *aab-dar* (bar man). I said a silent prayer of relief, as I had almost NOT ordered any ice, naively thinking the Kelvinator fridge would be adequate for any ice needed.

Post-brunch, the Captain, who was officiating Adjutant that day, was holding his mini-darbaar, long after the lunch was polished off, and the parachute canopy was taken down. Reading aloud a piece of *daak* (mail) , he said, triumphantly,

"Looks like we may have an incorrect use of an abbreviation in Regimental HQ correspondence !.'

Heads of all 3-stars, and below perked up.

It was very unlikely that our CO, who wrote the book, (actually MANY precis, user guides and instructor manuals) on service writing and formal correspondence, would, in a million years, let an incorrect use of abbreviation go uncorrected, on a document bearing his signature.

Was the well-chosen and highly regarded Typist NCO slipping his grip ? Could there be a chance to see him banished, and then c-a-r-e-f-u-l-l-y brought into one of our Squadron offices ? The prospects were opening up, as the Quartermaster and the Tech Adjutant started thinking a few cycles ahead, to ease their overburdened workloads.

'What is it ?' disbelievingly inquired another Captain, while slipping into his track top for the forthcoming basketball game.

'Look here', said the Captain, pointing out a letter 'See how 'canned' is abbreviated as 'cd' ?'

'Isn't that what it's supposed to be ?' said the QM.

'I bet it's not'... 'Youngster, what's the abbreviation for canned ?' he hollered at me

'Sir... um .. 'cnd' ?'

'You are bloody useless !'

Clearly no one knew for sure, so a runner was sent to the Regimental HQ, to get the much-thumbed service writing and abbreviation precis. By now there was an expectant crowd - neither knowing the correct abbreviation, nor wishing to give up an opportunity to see how this all shapes out.

Soon, the sweaty dispatch rider (DR) returned, the service abbreviation book snatched from his hands even before he could park his bike. Pages were turned, and lo and behold ... Canned was indeed spelled as 'cd'.

No words were exchanged, as the Captain who thought he had found an error in CO's drafting, slunk away, and we all decamped for evening sports. Peace returned to our corner of Punjab's hinterland.

CHAPTER 21 : NO SMALL POTATOES

To date, I do not know what his first name was. To me, to everyone at the Indian Military Academy (IMA), Dehradun, he was THE Company Commander to fear, and pray to God to NOT be assigned to his Company, Naushera. After coming from Echo squadron, the PT Squadron in NDA, I desperately wanted a 'chilled' out IMA company to spend my 12 months and pass out.(i.e. graduate, not collapse, as in US usage).

No such luck, as I found myself in Naushera Company - and the Company was located on prime real estate, in the British era Collins Block right in front of the main Chetwode building. In that block, my cabin was in the very front, highly visible row, which meant my cabin had to be in 'cabin cupboard' inspection-ready condition pretty much everyday.

Seniors of the previous course talked about the Company Commander in hushed tones - when they were not subjected to furious tongue lashings heard all over, as they scurried away from the Company Commander's Office. On any given day, he kept entire batches in varying states of hands-down, or quick 'putty parades' -timed, navy style dress changes. Also kept on their toes were the assorted Captains who served as Platoon Commanders , young Captains who themselves feared his wrath.

As the 1 year at IMA got over, I got commissioned, and a short while later, was with my unit participating in my very 1st Desert exercise, 'Bhavani Khadka', near the Indo-Pak border. It was after Holi, the exercise, which had gone on progressively since late Jan, was coming to an end.

Self-congratulatory back-patting was the mood that day, as various Units' Commandants, COs and others with shades of lipstick on their collar crowded up a *dhora* (hill) waiting for the GOC to come and congratulate them further.

To everyone's delight, snippets of intercepted radio telephony (RT) conversations violating prescribed norms, such as calling out names in clear, or using improper RT procedures were played on the PA system - supposedly to educate, but more to catch other units leaders in 'compromising RT positions'.

'Any concerns or areas of improvement?' asked the GOC, at the outset.

Silence - for all of 2 seconds.

'Yes sir', as a tall figure rose, fishing out something from his pockets, which turned out to be an onion and a potato.

'The quality of rations being supplied to the troops during the exercise is no good.'

Categorical statement ..... no beating about the bush.

Upon hearing this, the catering ASC Bn CO turned beetroot-red.

'This is what I picked up on the way in, and it is unacceptable'. The words and their tone was surprisingly familiar.

It was our own former Naushera Company Commander, Maj SB Konnur, now posted out of the Indian Military Academy, but with the same tough-to-please attitude, that we were seeing him dish out - except that this was happening before about 800 officers, of a fighting formation that had a frontline role in case of war.

The ASC Col spluttered and hemmed and hawed. Immediate reproach along with a bevy of orders were issued by the GOC, resulting in profuse sweating and saluting on the ASC Col's part. Any other mortal would have thought twice before turning the harsh spotlight under the desert sun, may be sent his thoughts in a letter later on - not Maj Konnur.

None of this was a surprise to him. He booked no compromises, shortcuts or excuses.

In another incident, I had 'checked myself' into the Military Hospital (MH) to avoid an end-of-term hike to Garhwa in the Himalayan mountains -something I would gladly pay for now, Many months back, I had foolishly volunteered, in a rush of bravado, but then developed cold-feet as valuable term break time drew nearer.

Word came to me, while admitted in the hospital, from someone who had reported sick that day, that Maj Konnur was going to get me relegated (moved to the next junior course). He had already hauled the senior term cadet appointments, as to how a junior under their care could call an ambulance and get himself admitted on his own. Hearing all this, I suddenly experienced a rapid recovery, setting in, and got myself discharged post-haste, and showing up at the Coy Cdr's office.

'Where the heck were you ? I will get you marched up today to the Commandant for relegation.' He said matter of factly, his eyes lighting up, as if he was taking me for an award ceremony. I presented myself and saluted stiffly, barking 'Good afternoon sir !'.

Gods of various shapes and denominations floated before my eyes.

Since 'Boldest action safest' has been a credo, I quickly gathered my wits, and proclaimed :

'Sir, I got myself discharged from the MH **specifically** to be here in time for the hike briefing. I think it's today. I am excited to go experience the Himalayas during the Term break.' came my exuberant reply, even though my heart was hammering inside my ribcage.'

He walked to within 6 inches of my face, gazing intently into my eyes. I looked back with joyously feigned excitement. After what seemed to be an eternity, he nodded, still not uttering a word, as his eyes continued to search my soul, for any sign of untruth.

Those words saved me, though he had gotten people to shed their term badges like a maple tree sheds leaves in autumn in Kashmir. Cadets 2 weeks from Passing out, but with 'modified' bed rest slips, found their term badges dropped after a scrutiny by Maj Konnur, for falsifying medical records - 1 week before their commissioning.

But then it was he - and only he - who stepped in, when a bunch of us made foolish choices in our choice-of-arms. No other Directing staff (DS) would have dared handhold his cadets from choosing arms or services they had a 'snowflake's chance in hell' of getting.

None would go to extraordinary lengths, get the choice-of-service forms brought from Chetwode Building, and sit 1:1 with us to review, and then amend our choices. Most Directing Staff (DS), are there to cherry-pick medalists and award winners for their own units, and the middle or lower merit cadets are usually left to their fate, with minimal guidance regarding such a fateful decision that will govern the next 20-30 years of their service in uniform.

We were the only lot that filled their choice-of-arms in pencil, then again filled them in pen, after being made aware of our 'real' chances and options - I doubt anyone else would dare go to such an extent to ensure his boys did not end up as square pegs in round holes.

When word came of his suffering a massive heart attack post retirement, while on the highway between Mysore and Bangalore, I was frozen and devastated. Sadly, he did not make it.

RIP sir..

I am sure the catering officer in heaven has ramped up the procurement procedures, and is furiously inspecting the potatoes and onions supplied - lest you march him up before Lord Vishnu himself.

CHAPTER 22: ICY FIRE IN MY HEART

When your school experience has you take on an icy lake of snow-melt seeping through hopelessly-inadequate and leaky Duckback shoes (which are meant for tropical rain, not Kashmir's winter), just to get to your class, you end up being able to take a lot of things in your stride. No pun intended.

A conventional school evokes vistas of solid buildings, quiet tree-lined avenues, massive libraries... Alas, those did not come my way for many years, as I did my 8th-10th at Army School Srinagar, in India's volatile Kashmir.

But this was no ordinary school, despite the shabby barracks that masqueraded as classrooms. Deep inside Srinagar's fortified Badami Bagh Cantonment, that too in pre-militancy Kashmir, it offered many unique vistas unseen by most schoolkids.

For starters, every school kid could make out the difference between the sound of a 7.62mm Self-loading rifle (SLR) round, a 9 mm carbine,, a Browning or a Berretta pistol, and the occasional staccato of a Light Machine gun (LMG) – standard issue firearms fired almost non-stop at a nearby firing range.

Barbed wire fencing around the campus had empty rusty cans strung on them - to detect intruders. Massive TATRA trucks would unload tanks and Infantry Combat Vehicles, like cement bags are unloaded in civilian areas.

But the big picture was even more stunning – The school was overlooked by Nanga Parbat, situated in Pakistani Kashmir, also called 'Killer Mountain', yet visible from Indian Kashmir. So tall that despite the 80 miles (130 km) and a hot border, it could be seen popping its head over to the North, across hundreds of peaks in Kashmir's northern wilderness.

Long before 'Rambo III" introduced the world to the lethality of helicopter gunships, especially the massive, heavily armoured Mi-24 'Hind' helicopter gunships, nicknamed Crocodile, we would readily perk up at the distinctive heavy sound of its 1,700 HP twin Isotov engines, as it would lift off, bristling with weaponry and armed troops, we were well .

It would make lazy passes low over the school, as they came into land at Srinagar's helipad, and it wasn't uncommon to know the pilots and their kids, who studied with uss.. Since I lived in a Kashmiri civilian neighborhood, pro-Pakistani kids would cheer *'Pakistan ne humla bola'* (Pakistan has attacked (to free Kashmir)), little caring about the Indian roundels on the gunships.

As students, we were a known entity to the troops and were often waved through, while riding our bicycles in those pre-militancy days. On Baisakhi Day (Apr 13th, 1984), as I pedaled by the Corps Commander's residence, en route to pluck some apples off the Kashmir Maharaja's estate, I did not had any clue that India had launched an operation in the icy peaks of Siachen glacier, where to this day, they hold the higher ground, despite sneaky attempts to squander precious tactical advantage in the name of 'demilitarization'.

Now, as geopolitics in Kashmir, Gilgit-Baltistan and other areas becomes more complex, such days are remnants of past innocence. Now, as Chinese contingents parade on Pakistan's national day parade, the chances of any territorial concessions are next to nothing.

Back in the mid-80s, Gupkar Road would have Kashmir's dethroned playboy Chief Minister, mocked as Kashmir's 'wazeer-e-disco', riding on his Yamaha 350 motorbike, with a Bollywood art movie actress in tow, both otherwise married. Such are the men we appointed to guard our most strategic state, in a naked powerplay that would soon set the Valley aflame, after a hideously rigged election in 1987.

A 100 m away from the school's perimeter, massive Czech Tatra tank transporters would be lined up. Their heavy diesels, as they loaded and unloaded tanks, despite Kashmir's mountainous terrain, would overcome everyone with heady diesel fumes, but no one complained.

Back in 1962, Sino-Indian war, India disassembled French made AMX-13 tanks belonging to 20th Lancers,, loaded them on to Russian AN-12 and deployed them at 14,000 ft elevation at Chushul, on the Chinese front, in sub-zero conditions of late October with Ladakh's harsh winter settling in – thereby re-writing conventional military wisdom that tanks are meant for flat terrains.

Even in the 80s, India would not lower its guard, as the flat valley of Kashmir has many use cases to deploy tanks, if and when the time comes. As a result of this action, Chinese forces were held off at the Spanggur gap, which fell to the enemy, but India managed to hold on to Chushul itself, with significant implications for its defence.

Since schools in Kashmir have a long winter, and a short summer, they are at a disadvantage to the plains, where the course is already started in the 1st couple of weeks before summer break. Here, we were lucky to get textbooks by Oct. That too, we had to go deep into interior Srinagar, to a single shop across miles of hostile neighborhoods, with scruffy street kids in dark shaded 'pherans' itching to lay hands on an 'Indian' schoolboy.

One fine day, the school got a contingent of European fair-skinned, blue eyed kids. They were the children of the staff at the UN Mission in Kashmir, whose job was to monitor the ceasefire line in Kashmir, but it did little on ground, given India's focus on not allowing the UN any role in a bilateral conflict. Their lunch on a grassy strip, with packaged cheese, canned Coca Cola and other assorted goodies made them feel watched from a distance. Later, to appear neutral, and not study in an Army-funded school, they were moved to a Civilian missionary school.

'The more you sweat in peace, the less you bleed in war', has long been a military adage. For us, the gravelly football fields, without a blade of grass, in ironically one of the greenest places on Earth, meant we bled more than we sweated, in a sport where the ball was ignored, and scores settled by landing kicks on oppositions' shins by heavy military DMS boots purloined from shoe racks of the schoolkids' Officer dads, with the approval of their trusted Batman (an aide, not the comic hero). Hideous tuck shop samosas, meant for troops, at a cheap 7 for 2 Rupees, were a treat, despite their griminess, and orders to not partake them.

To get to the school, from my neighborhood adjoining the cantonment, I, and a few other civilian students, would be riding their bicycles on the busy National Highway 1A (NH1A), weaving through convoys of heavy military trucks resupplying outposts. Also sharing roadspace would be civilian 'Matador' vans, from one of which the daughter of a future Chief Minister, who also went on to occupy the chair, once militancy raised its head.

En route, I became friends with the sole supplier of milk to Kashmir, who would bring in a tanker every day, and unload it at a point which was again the last safe place for Indian trucks to come in. Given the ease with which supplies could be interdicted, my 14-year old brain was quick to capitalize on the need to be friendly with the 'capo di tuti capi' of Kashmir's milk supply. Given the harsh winters, cattle from the plains couldn't be raised in the cold Valley, so the milk would be shipped from far off Amritsar or Mukerian, and the arrival of the tanker would be a welcome affair. Tribal cattlemen from places like Baramullah would then take large milk cans, and load them on their horsecarts. How much milk got spoiled due to any delay caused by landslides, or civil unrest, can only be guessed.

The irony of mobs stoning, and even burning trucks bringing in milk for their infants, and then complaining about it, is something that may seek strange – but Kashmir has a long pattern of resources that sustain and make life easier, being mysteriously set ablaze or destroyed otherwise, due to them coming in from 'India'. That destruction would then be attributed to security forces or the Establishment, and then be put to use for propaganda purposes – be in milk trucks, or electricity transformers being sabotaged.

Many of the school alums did surprisingly well – going on to solid professions, many rising to the top in the civilian and military professions, and some of us landing overseas, where we now have classmates in places such as Silicon Valley, Florida, Vancouver and New York. The most cherished are those who laid down their lives, in the prime of their youth, serving the nation.So, while we never got to finish our syllabus; there was enough learning. Compared to public schools in Delhi, so laid back was the teaching there, that I did not learn that one needed to prepare for practicals, till I got to a school in Delhi, where my lack of preparation made me the cynosure of silent criticism, as I asked my new classmates how they prepared for the lab - and got cold stares instead, at my lack of awareness.

But then who cared, as I was back in 'India' then.

CHAPTER 23 : 'KNEEL BEFORE THE GREAT LEADER !'

Close to Diwali a few years back, it felt as if all hell was breaking loose and my business trip to Beijing was already morphing into a miserable odyssey from the get go. Nothing major, just a series of annoyances piling up..

To begin with even a diluted Diwali abroad, in the US, is still Diwali, and while I am OK with business travel, I was annoyed that the on-site team was not willing to RTFM (Read the 'f&^%ing' Manual), and insisted on our team to fly down and train them, that too at the 11th hour, which happened to be the week of Diwali.

It almost became a modern day 'Boxer Rebellion', (if the Academy bouts are considered). The Beijing airport custom person, beamed his widest 'dental-work-needed' smile at the *gora* (white) team members, ahead of me, but scowled and,- believe it or not - took out a tiny magnification glass to look at my Chinese visa ('Yeah, I am simply dying to disappear in your nation'), on my Indian passport. I scowled back.

He then beckoned a supervisor, and they both went over my visa stamp. Since, in desi fashion, I had used an earlier used, once-recycled photo at the last minute, for my Chinese visa, it did not meet their approval. Head shakes and nay-sayings followed, and I too stood glowering.

After eternity, he flicked an imaginary spec of dust from my pic, and handed it back. I had noticed he specifically pulled out the page across the US visa, and scrawled all over it with extra ink.

I too, in a flash of annoyance, wiped the excessive red ink off the fresh red stamp, going out of my way to clean up my US visa stamp on the opposite page from any Chinese ink.

He went crimson with rage. Maybe he would stop my entry, and have me turn back, or so I thought. No such luck, as our clumsy 'handler' dive-rolled in between, and took me away. I too was not willing to take this crap as *'hum bhi khaate peete ghar ke hain'*, (we too hail from a solid background) and that too crap from the Sugar-sector *waalas* !.. Naah !

During the technical training, on the next generation Intel products, they too would wheel me out before crowds of tech media - something which was to be done by their team.

More silent rage. The icing was that invariably, after my talk, some guy would come and ask me 'Are you with the product team ?' trying to find an 'American' engineer to answer their questions. Even after I had patiently gone over it, instead of thanks, it would be followed by 'You have good technical knowledge' or 'Your English is very nice, but you are from India !', leaving me marveling at their ignorance and the backhanded compliment I had just got as reward for helping him out with a bunch of questions.

On the final weekend, a trip to Tiananmen Square was arranged - Ground Zero and the site of a bloody student crackdown during June 1989. For some reason, the People's Liberation

Army (PLA), does not think much of having army barracks put up in the unlikeliest of places, such as amidst a complex of 5-star hotels, where foreign visitors like me were staying.

One could see them from the 14th floor of the hotel, doing some form of Kung Fu (it was always a martial art performance on display). Even in the Forbidden Palace, and despite all the hype, I had seen more riches in palaces of erstwhile states like Banaras, than the Forbidden Palace, and there, incongruously, was a was a barrack and chin up bars in the middle of the Imperial Palace.

Fittingly, it was next to 'Wu Men Gate', which as legend has it, was the equivalent of Traitor's Gate of Tower of London, but backwards, i.e. it would be the gate through which Nobility would exit before meeting an executioner's blade.

As I survived my own exit from the Gate, a glowering portrait of Chairman Mao drilled its gaze into me. I was visualizing where the demonstrator who blocked the tank column stood etc. It was about 5 PM, close to sunset, and hence Retreat time

Some of the tallest, square jawed Han soldiers were doing their drill movements at the base of a courtyard size giant flagpole. As they began playing their version of Taps, a bevy of Military Police, batons in hand, fanned out.

Almost immediately, about 3,000-4,000 Chinese gathered there, got on their knees and bowed before the flag, a collective, low moan rising above them. I now realized why a bunch of Western tourists were hustled away by their guide, to a distant spot. Lo and behold, I found myself being yelled at, amidst a sea of kneeling Chinese, and gestures and expressions being directed my way.

Since a flag deserves respect, not obsequious tribute, I had stood at attention, with my right hand across my heart, US-style. But that was apparently not enough. Soon a guard got into my face, making repeated gestures to kneel.

I shook my head, as his superior also fetched up. I pointed to my small lapel pin with the Indian flag on it. The superior spoke English.

I told him that I respect the flag, and am an ex-Indian Army, and I cannot bow before it as I am not from China. A few 100 eyes were following this discussion.

As a face-saver, I offered to move to the rear of the crowd. He agreed, breathing a sigh of relief. We walked back, flanked Flag Corporal style, heading away from a clearly-disapproving Mao-saheb.

Soon the ceremony began. It was a ceremony full of flourishes, and Soviet-esque drill movements. As the flag came down, we realized the solemnity of the moment, shaking hands as we departed, never to meet again.

CHAPTER 24 : MAKING A TRAIN MOVE

'Sir ! Brigade se tasking aayi hai !'

(Sir ! We have received a task assignment from the Brigade HQ)

These 6 words have the power to mess up the well laid plans of Regimental routine, spiking the 2 I/C's bone soup lunch, or the Adjutant's plans for some afternoon shut eye, all in a matter of a couple of seconds. But since orders from up above are meant to be followed with utmost diligence, the chain of authority and command kicks in, and all incoming series of orders are ingested, processed and digested, and military machinery hums on.

Unbeknownst to this word of impending flurry of activity coming my way, I was warming myself by the open wood stove, sitting in the Squadron *'langar'* (mess hall for troops), eyeing the thickening, bubbling 50-litre vat of aromatic *'rajma-chawal'* (kidney beans and rice), and an accompanying container full of rice *kheer* for dessert. Moments separated me from my God-given Young Officer duty to sample this delight, all in the name of troop welfare of course, as the mess NCO looked on for my approval. Only the dignity of the stars on my shoulders kept me from drooling right there.

Dalbir, the dispatcher's 350 cc Royal Enfield motorcycle sputtered to a halt outside the mess hall, as he dismounted and strode briskly towards me, soaked in sweat in the heat.

" How hard do these dispatch riders work all day !", I thought.

Salutes were exchanged, and he asked me to come with him to the Regimental HQ (RHQ), immediately, as the Adjutant was looking for me. My concern for Dalbir's fatigue evaporated like the steam from that cauldron of *kheer* in the background, and my prospects of sampling a bowl or a ladle, along with it.

Since it was still 30 min before my daily Inquisition before the Adjutant, I could not feel good about what must have happened. It could be one of many scenarios...

A week before, I had started a T-72 tank, and then carelessly left it idling for 10 min, as the pre-course class took a break.I was quickly hauled to task, being reminded by the Training Daffadar (NCO) as to how *'impaartant'* a tank's engine hours (hours spent when the engine is running), and track hours (hours when the tank actually moves on its tracks) are in its lifespan, and to NEVER let it run unless absolutely necessary.

His words were a manifestation of experience learned, and paid for, in human blood.

Experienced Junior Commissioned Officers (JCOs, who are the equivalent of Staff Sergeants and other enlisted men's leaders in the US), would tell me that the regiment had fought for 3 days straight during 1971 Indo-Pak war, in the Battle of Basantar, and old timers told the instances where the crew threw out everything, including dry rations, just to stock their Vijayanta tanks with all the ammunition, spares, fuel jerrycans and lubricants they could get, just to keep on fighting till the battle was over.

Death came to tank crews -own or enemy's - which had the misfortune of breaking down amidst battle, or those whose weaponry failed, or ran out of tank rounds to fire, and being picked off at a distance, perishing as human torches.

So such battle wisdom had to be imbibed, irrespective of whether it came from an Officer or an enlisted man, without any arrogance of being a junior officer and him being an NCO. In fact, woe betide the young officer who foolishly indulged in brash behavior with the troops. Word of that would travel, in real time, to the Regimental HQ, and lead to severe admonishment and corrective guard check punishments, where you go on the stroke of the hour, at every hour after midnight to see if the various guard posts were in fact alert.

It was early March and the Unit was preparing to go for annual Field exercises to the Rajasthan deserts. To those not familiar with Indo-Pakistani border terrain, a quick primer...

Long before the artillery guns have pounded each other's positions in the icy wastes of the Siachen, from 1984, the Desert front is where the make or break battles have been, and will be fought, in the vast empty sands of Rajasthan state, bordering the Southern Punjab region of Pakistan.

The desert unifies the 2 warring nations, esp. in the area that stretches from Suratgarth in Northern Rajasthan, to Jaisalmer in the South West, with Pakistan's forces concentrated in garrisons like Fort Abbas and Pano Aquil, with India lodged in Suratgarh, Bhatinda and other towns and garrisons.

As and when 'the balloon will go up', in theory and doctrine, in a conventional war, this is where India's meaty forearm will reach across the open sands, wrap itself around Pakistan's narrow waistline at the Indus river, and apply pressure, irrespective of anything the enemy can throw in conventional warfare, or even nuclear, if it came to that.

Hence it's in the deserts that forces train, practically all year round, even though open spaces of 100s of sq km needed for tank training comes under the plough or is built up, making open spaces scarcer every year, pushing troops deeper in the desert, and towards the border.

The 'tasking' that had come was in the form of go ahead to load the tanks on the rail cars that would carry the unit's tanks to the exercise area by Bikaner, in the Rajasthan Desert An empty train rake was supposed to be ready and waiting at nearby Nabha station. Most north Indian towns with cantonments have permanent sidings where tanks can simply roll onto special flatcars, as and when they need to be mobilized to turn their guns towards our errant sibling across the border.

' Youngster, make haste to the station. Await orders. Capt 'Phil Collins' would be getting there.', stated the Adjutant, as soon as I showed up.

Capt 'Phil Collins' was a tough task master, but fair, and a great mentor. His resemblance to the famous singer was not in his voice, but his prematurely balding pate, a fact that he rued mournfully, given his continued bachelorhood, much to everyone else's delight. Great guy, who was taken away too soon by fate.

! hopped on to a tarp-less Shaktiman 3-ton truck that had seen better days, as it stood baking in the sun for 45 min, awaiting my arrival, complete with the joyful countenance of men who had been told to wolf down their lunch and be ready to move out for an afternoon of toil.

We rolled out of the cantonment en route to the station. Once out, the men set in place a well-worn routine. As we approached a roadside fruit seller, word was passed that the men were thirsty. This, when we had left the unit lines not even 10 min back. I expected this, but pretended to play along, asking the driver to stop at the fruit stand, and buying a sackful of oranges and *kinnoo*. Pretty soon, the 6-foot Sikhs and Dogras would be squeezing orange peels in each other's eyes, like school kids, till a few Punjabi words from the JCO in charge had them on their way.

In Punjabi, verbal abuse is not abuse, but earthy grammar, almost a manifestation of loving care, so no one really minds.

Reaching Nabha station, a picture of a rural idyll awaited me. It has a single track towards Bhatinda, and a couple of rail sidings. A parked row of flat cars, and other assorted wagons stood alongside, but they were on the wrong track, away from where the loading ramp track was. To make things worse, the tank flat cars lay sandwiched among freight cars, as if the rake had been assembled at the last minute, without putting the flat cars at one end, to allow loading of tanks

Only a locomotive sent by the railways, from either Patiala or Ambala, at the discretion of their masters would at some point, show up and remedy the situation. Railways rolling stock does not get any revenue from military traffic, so they are in no rush to help - except when war breaks out, at which time, the best resources are made available, post-haste.

The men were now horsing around at the station water pump, dousing each other with mugfuls of cold water.Since it was not in my pay grade to do anything about the non-ready state of the flat cars, I let them be.

Soon, Capt Phil would join us, but he would probably address the forefathers and mothers of the railway staff, in choicest Punjabi, and then we would need to head back to the Unit and report.. Probably miss the evening PT if we were lucky.

Lo and behold, Capt Phil's meticulously maintained jeep screeched to a halt, and calm descended in a hush. The men snapped to attention, formed up instantly... Gone was the hilarity, and the firm face of front line troops took over, cast in stone, in the blink of an eye. The Captain had been with the unit for a few years, and the men knew him and his result-orientedness well, and respected his experience.

' Sir .. the power has not yet arrived' I spoke up, stating the obvious.

'So...?' was his reply. ' What do you think needs to be done ?'

' Have the station master call up Patiala or Ambala and send a diesel ? Otherwise how can we even have the flatcars set right ?'

His jaw dropped at my naivete, but he burst out laughing.

' No, WE (gesturing to all of us in a 360 degree motion of his index finger), will take care of it. The CO is coming in a couple of hours, and the train will leave tonight, with tanks loaded'

'He can't be serious !' I thought. What on earth can be done with 1,000s of tons of immobile mass parked on the tracks ?

But to my amazement, a column of dust rose from the unit's direction, as the clanking of tank tracks and roar of T72s on the move came in our direction. Instead of waiting for the tanks to be loaded on Tatra transporters, and then unloaded at the station, Capt Phil had simply opened the garages, and ordered them to drive alongside the road for the 3 odd km to the station. Something which would usually be allowed only in wartime or an emergency, and that too with the Civil authorities permission, was completely sidelined by his goal-oriented thinking.

I looked at the incongruous sight of a tank rounding the corner, gun barrel barely missing a roadside *jalebi* stand by a whisker, a storm of flies lifting off the syrupy jalebis piled up.

But the tank column was on the other side of the railway tracks and the embarkation ramp, and in the absence of a proper grade crossing, it would be impossible to simply drive them over the steel rails and cross over - they would buckle like twigs, snapping a strategic national link to the border.

A party of 8-10 men peeled towards the tracks, and immediately began digging the hard soil next to them with a vengeance. Soon enough, loose dirt was piled up, burying the tracks in a mud crossing about 10 feet wide, and 10 inches deep, forming a ramp for the tanks to cross the railway line. This takes the pressure a free-standing rail would take, and the tank can negotiate the train track with no damage

'But what are we gonna do now?', I thought, as about 6 freight cars lay between the leading tank and the 1st available flatcar. Surely we can't lift the cars magically.

Again, I was woefully out of touch about how things are done in a world where 'No' is not an option.

The station master was summoned, and the situation explained. When he protested, Capt Phil had a quiet word with him, and his demeanor suddenly changed, and became cooperative. I might have caught a glimpse of a couple of rum bottles changing hands, but I could be hallucinating at that point.

Parties of men positioned themselves next to the rail cars, as a railway staffer disconnected the intervening cars. Since these too needed to be a part of the military train, they had to be re-coupled back in a precise order.

With a heave-ho, the men began pushing individual rail cars, which were now detached, no locomotive anywhere in sight. I could not believe what I was seeing.

We began pushing individual cars, across the main line, and onto another track. When an express train came barreling through, every one stopped, and points reset, in a very 'Five Man Army' manner, as the train was led through a gap between the detached coaches on either side of the rail fork, much to the amazement of the train's crew.

Soon enough, like ants on a piece of egg-on-toast, the men had split up the freight cars, and then pushed the lead flat car, clearing the access to the front of the loading ramp. No sooner had the ramp clanged on to the concrete, the first tank rumbled on, making its way to the furthest flat car. A 20-year old *sowar* (tank trooper) barely out of training, skillfully guiding another 20-year old driver gunning the tank merrily as if he were driving a tractor on a farm.

Age has nothing to do with it, as it's only the best men who are chosen to guide the tank driver via hand signals, as barely a couple of inches of margin is there between the tank and the edge of the rail car, coupled with zero visibility for the driver. It doesn't matter if they are barely out of their teens. Their skill and the faith of their team makes it work. Lots of precision and cool nerves are needed to prevent a 45 ton behemoth from toppling over to the tracks below.

To say that we were drenched in sweat would be an understatement. A game of squash leaves you drenched, and this was a different ball game altogether. As the last tank rolled on, we heard a locomotive's sound from one direction, and saw the CO's Gypsy pull in from the other.

Startled looks followed, in a familiar sequence, mainly from the locomotive crew. With the loaded tanks, no way could the train be pushed by a few men anymore, so the arrival of the locomotive was a God-send. Soon it stood coupled facing towards the desert, idling away.

The CO merely said 'Good job' to Capt Phil, and his complete trust in him was clear from his manner by which his expectation of the train being ready was met. The CO was off in a cloud of dust, minutes later.

Soon the loaded train was pulled back a bit, and the remaining wagons inserted in between the flat cars and the locomotive. 'Hand shunting' was a new phrase in my vocabulary.

My hopes of being on the train when it left were soon dashed. Vistas of me approving the trains move through Rajasthan's mustard fields, as a stiff breeze pulled at my starched 'patka' face cover evaporated.

I and another Lieutenant were now going to cycle the 150 km from Nabha to the Exercise area beyond Suratgarh. Unlike the Concorde Pro 10 cycle with the CO, I had a mid-size, ungeared bicycle with an uncomfortable seat, borrowed from a school age cousin. But paddle along we did, passing through Sangrur, Barnala and Bhatinda. It actually turned out to be quite a memorable experience for me.

En route, a General's vehicle headed to the exercise area came to a halt on seeing this 'induction by bicycle' and prompt refreshments arranged from his Rover. My NDA Wing Division Officer was now a Staff Officer, to the General, and it was quite a moment to reconnect with him after 4 years, with me no longer a cadet. He beamed proudly at me, and talked well about my attitude during training, which was news to me.

Sandstorms greeted us after we crossed Suratgarh, making further progress on bicycles towards Lunkaran Sar impossible. So we loaded our cycles, and tired bums into a jolty 3-tonner, and completed the remaining induction, similarly uncomfortable, if not more, due to a complete lack of suspension in the truck as it bounced off the broken roads.

The next few days would have me learn from some of the best, most experienced officers in desert warfare, but Day 1 leading to exercise had been memorable.

As an officer, you get the job done - something that comes in handy to this day, long after the civilian attire has taken over.

CHAPTER 25 : WHERE TO DINE ?

It has always struck me as a bit tragic, the the 1857 Revolt (1st War of Indian Independence), was put down by the British with the help of hurriedly raised garrisons of Pathans, Sikhs, and Gorkhasbarely a few 1000 in number - Not only that, a few years further back, the British had been in the fight of their lives with each of these warrior groups .

As 1857 and its cataclysmic events approached, the Indian sub-continent saw new alliances form between those who fought each other, and the British not long back. The Gurkhas had been defeated in the Anglo-Nepal War (1814-16) and the Treaty of Sugauli had been signed/imposed. The Sikhs 'Khalsa fauj' had been defeated even more recently, at the Battle of Chillianwala in 1849, a mere 8 years before the revolt.

And the Frontier Pathan tribesmen have never really been aligned with anyone, ever, till present day - yet all 3 of these ethnic groups, with well documented histories of multi-generational rivalries, and feuds, would join a much smaller, British-led garrison, and set out to crush the rebellion of their countrymen.

In the case of the Sikh soldiery joining the British, the reason could be that in the Anglo-Sikh Wars, the British had their Native Bengal Infantry staffed by *'purabiyas'* (men from Indo-Gangetic plains, who spoke Hindi and hailed from so-named United Provinces (present state of *Uttar Pradesh*) along with those from the Central Provinces, present day *Madhya Pradesh* state), and when the British won, the *Purabiyas* reportedly were either corrupt, or ill-treated, or extorted from the Sikh peasantry - a fact not forgotten by their victims.

So when the time came to battle with the same *Purabiyas* leading the revolt from Merrut and Barrackpore, the Sikhs were ready to band under the exotically named *'Be-tarteeb Risalas'* - or 'Irregular Horse', which were hurriedly raised, flying columns of horsemen, formed in undivided Punjab, and galloping non-stop, to rally to the cause of the Company Bahadur - ready to unsheath their swords and bay for some Purabiya blood. They were also joined with Pathan and tribal horsemen from Peshawar and other Frontier towns in present-day Pakistan, as nothing excited a Pathan more than the prospect of fighting, and pillaging.

The rest is history ...Kunjpura... Badli Ki Sarai, Kashmere Gate were locations of pitched battles, where slowly the needle moved towards the British forces suppressing the revolt.

Could the British ever have won India, had the 3 largest fighting groups not rallied under their banner - That would, in theory, have meant Indian independence 90 years earlier ?

Cut to 1994

For me, getting commissioned into a very traditional unit, brought this aspect front and center, on a daily basis. The Unit (Hodson's Horse), remains the ONLY Indian Army Unit that has somehow managed to continue to be named after its British Founder, Maj. WSR Hodson, long after other British-raised Unit's like Skinner's Horse have been renamed as 1H.

And since any Nazi-inspired significance is never on anyone's horizon, brass insignia with 'H.H.' written on them are par for course, and not to be taken as salutation to Herr Hitler.

... and Hodson was no ordinary person, as he, with a few shots of his Victoria Carbine, in Delhi's *Khooni Darwaza* (Bloody Gate), executed the last 3 sons of the ailing Mughal Emperor, Bahadur Shah Zafar. Of course, these 3 deceased also had been accused of massacring English women and children in Delhi, so *karma* is a shot that does go around, and hits you.

The said Victoria carbine held centerplace in the richly endowed Officers Mess, flanked by a pair of gargantuan Elephant tusks (I took them to be mammoth tusks), with a khaki tunic clad portrait of its former owner looking out in the distance.

A key rite of passage, and acceptance, is passing the dreaded Silver test, where the 2nd Lieutenant is expected to conduct a Senior Major around the Mess, with the facts, dates, titles about every trophy rolling off his tongue around various pieces of assorted silverware lying about.

This is the ticket to finally getting acceptance in the Unit, it's importance cannot be over-emphasised, It is OK to have not cleared the promotion Part B exams, even as a Captain, but woe betide those who had not cleared the Silver test.

Queries like

-Who was 'Khan Saheb' Mir Zafar Khan Sardar Bahadur (a long deceased Subedar)...

-How many medals for Africa's Battle of Suakin were won by the Unit (I think it was 14 or 16).

-Who are the soldiers cast in sterling Silver on that trophy (A Punjabi Mussalman, a Pathan, a Dogra..) ,

-What's the connection with Pakistan's Probyn's Horse, India's Scinde Horse and Hodson's Horse (they all exchanged a Squadron upon Independence, as respective soldiers opted for India or Pakistan)

Such questions can be expected to rain down should there be nothing exciting on the TV, and a fresh-from-posting Major Saab is back in the Unit, sizing you up, before the first egg-n-toast crumbs hit your shirt front.

But meals had to be had ... and in a sleep deprived regimen of PT, Drill, learning the tank's innards, left little time to be had to enjoy the meal in Officers Mess.

A survival plan was resorted to .. one that many would have done in similar situations I am sure.

As a young officer, it is important that you check in on your mens' living conditions, occasionally sampling the food being cooked in Squadron langars (kitchens)... the 'A' and 'B'

Squadrons were Jatt Sikhs from the Amritsar- Taran Tarn belt, the 'C' squadron was Dogras from Himachal and erst while Hill states..and the cuisine was all-around marvellous.

Breakfast would be had, not by having the Officer Mess NCO serve a well-made omelette, but by ducking into 'A' squadron's langar, and gulping down scalding hot '*poori sabzi*' (puffed fried bread with curried vegetables) .. frantically hushing the langar staff into silence, lest they start off with 'Saavdhans' (Attentions)... a fistful of fragrant, and extremely hot halwa later, I would have disappeared, having saved 20 min, and be ready and changed for the day.

For lunch, I would dive alternately into B or C Squadron langars - the sallow complexioned Sikhs would be gazing with their eyes deep in their recessed sockets, as to where '*saheb-ji*' is heading. In the delicately choreographed world of inter-squadron rivalry, an Officer cannot be seen as frequenting a particular kitchen for long, lest there be '*langar gup*' (gossip) and loose talk about favoritism.

That left dinner, which is where one would have been most vulnerable to be keeping company to some forced bachelor downing his rum. A quick breezy entry through the main door, acknowledging a flurry of salutes, preferably just after the evening guard had taken over. A quick hello to someone already there ... and then out the backdoor where the head cook would have laid out the 1st servings for that night.

A few bites of that, and back to the room, where my *sahayak* (helper) would have kept a large flask of creamy-yellow milk from Punjab's famed dairies.A glass of it would be potent enough to knock you over into deep sleep.

And so I did this for a few days, with being a teetotaller and all keeping everyone guessing that I was on the 'other' side of Mess... till I made the classic mistake of assassination victims - I fell into a pattern.

The *poori-subji*, the badam-flavored *halwa*, the cuts of grilled *kaleji*, and the overall efficiency had me hooked. Unbeknownst to me a couple of off-hand inquiries pretty much laid bare my culinary shenanigans to the Adjutant.

Needless to say, I was under the mat - and at the dining table for hours in advance, for days to come. In no time, the Silver test was memorized, and narrated before a feline-like Maj. Sekhon. Thankfully, I passed in my 1st attempt, which brought another set of challenges from other Young Officers still in the process of attempting it.

Those long-lost Pathan, Sikh and other warriors, who had borne arms under the Union Jack in 1857, and crushed the 1st battle of Indian Independence, would now be gazing fixedly, upon me as I stood for hours,with a carefully nursed rum, and a sweltering collar in Punjab's July humidity, hearing yet another analysis of 'Schindler's List' for the nth time.

CHAPTER 26 : SHORTCUTS & MUDDY BOOTS

It was the day after New Years, and I had just joined the unit at Nabha. The day before, Navjot Singh Sidhu, the motormouth cricketer had hitched a ride perched on my rolled bedroll as he arrived at the last minute, without a reservation in the AC coach of the Delhi-Bhatinda Intercity. The Senior subaltern had shown me my room in the 'Stables', the quarters for young cavalrymen such as yours truly. Life was great...

The party was on at full-blast with Karishma Kapoor's latest song 'Neeli Neeli aankhey meri ...' threatening to rip the aging fabric of the Brigade mess curtains.

After a rollicking party lasting till 3-4 AM, true to form, there was a mandatory 5 km Battle Physical Endurance Training (BPET), a 5 km run in battle rig, to be run at 6 AM on Jan 1.

Into the Nabha fog we went, with me actually not being too thrilled at running with an Armored Corps officer issued weapon choice of a 9mm carbine or a 9 mm pistol. Unlike the Self Loading Rifle (SLR) used at IMA BPET, which comfortably lodges itself on your shoulder, and stays there, the carbine or the pistol, despite their light weight, actually proved cumbersome while hitting stride.

Anyway, I was comfortably in the lead as we took the final turn on the periphery road. I was trying hard to run non-chalantly, aware that the men I was running with could effortlessly out run me.

Around the perimeter of the cantonment in Nabha, ran a barbed wire fence with a drainage channel (nala), about 5-6 feet wide. As we approached the entry gate, I saw from the corner of my eye, a pair break off into the swirly fog, and cut across the nala and into a gap in the wire, ultimately rejoining the running groups ahead - in effect, taking a short-cut.

I made a mental note of it, and realized that I needed to show up with a good time, as everyone would be looking out for how I did.

Once the run was done, the participating officers and troops re-assembled on the sports field. The CO had got word of some troops taking a short cut, almost as soon as the race was over.

'The CO will want to know who took a shortcut' whispered by senior Sub. For sure, the run would be canceled and everyone would be required to repeat it, to ensure its integrity.

I began thinking about how to separate those characters. I knew these guys were from 'C' Squadron, as they were Dogras in a unit with Dogras and Sikh troops, seen as they were without the patka that Sikh troops don for sports. My modus operandi would be to have them get a chance to own up, and if none stepped forward, then walk up to the 'Satisfactory' enclosure, have them fall-in, do a khuli-line chal (open formation), and walk behind them. Having run through the nala, they would have fresh mud on their boots.

To an ex-NDA, nothing would show me up in a macho light, than say if I took a SLR from one of the troops, and walked right behind the defaulters and nudged them with the rifle-butt to 'step out' ?

But what would happen then ?

Were they men whose leave was held up because of BPET? One of them had made eye contact with me, and knew I had been on to them. The other was panting even though the run ended 10 min back. Clearly these guys had issues, and would not have cleared the event fair and square.

But what to do ?

Confusing me further was the prevailing sentiment since Academy days, where we sort our problems by ourselves, without going 'official' about it. Not a perfect scenario in current man management practices, but these were not the days about all that new thinking.

We all despised 'put up types' (snitches) right from the Academy days - and I had run 21 restrictions rather than finger anyone, for ordering a heat session on the hot tiles at NDA.

'Sir, the youngster has run with them, he would know' said the 2IC.

Suddenly, I was the cynosure of all eyes. I felt as if I had taken the shortcut instead. Do I become an eagle-eyed 'Keen Kumar', and announce my presence on Day 1 ?

I cleared my throat and said that I was running ahead and the fog was preventing any good view, but I did hear commotion behind, which I took to the men urging each other, so it could well have been someone taking the short cut.

The CO promptly ordered the run cancelled. But I felt a relief, not because I was not being in a spotlight, but because, in the fairness of things in the Service, in addition to those who took the shortcut, the culpability also resided with those who ran with them - men who had stayed silent. And it is better for the entire lot to go on the run again, than let anyone condone shortcuts.

The 2 men came back to me and swore they would not do it again. I immediately had them come for afternoon runs for the next week, as remedial measures had to be taken.. All unofficial of course.

Even now, when I do see events taking place in the organizations in the civilian world, be it a status report that does not completely share the complete picture, I do make it a point to not criticize the owner, but go out of my way to poke holes in it, so they end up doing it again... for better most of the times.

Muddy boots can't be allowed after all.

CHAPTER 27 : CRIME & PUNISHMENT

The constant pressure during training at the various services Academies often causes cadets to bemoan their confines, not unlike an open prison, at least to some 'frisky' types ... At a superficial level, it does give that impression - it's nestled in a bowl shaped valley, about 10,000 acres or so, with few ingress and egress points...A massive dam runs on one flank,one which notoriously gave way in the 60s, and one, in whose reservoir, recent news indicates there is now a population of crocodiles introduced in the dam's lake, by the Navy, to deter trespassers.

As though the cumulative misery wasn't enough to blow Lady Luck's snot out in your face.....

But more apt is the fact that just like in a prison, the prisoners watch every move of their guards, and the overall system, for signs of weaknesses, and tend to exploit them at the first available opportunity, and not get caught... Because then, you have to fall on your sword and do the honorable thing of owning up... and get more official and unofficial punishments for this fresh transgression..

Since the leadership of the Academy rotates at the Lt. Gen rank amongst Army, Navy and Air Force senior officers, the 'heat' in the Academy also undergoes cyclical changes... Army Commandants are noted to be tough and aggressive and that percolates through like a leaky jam sandwich on a hot summer day.

A Mughal-era fort, Sinhagad (Lion's Fortress), looks over the valley benignly from about 22 km away.. Site of a gory battle, it was won by Maratha Chieftain Shivaji, through his able lieutenant, Tanaji Malsure, who, legend has it, used a monitor lizard (Goh) named Yashwanti, to act as a grapnel to scale the fort from its most challenging direction, and in the process laying down his life, causing Shivaji to lament 'garh aala pun singh geyla' (We won the fort but lost the lion), and rename it from Kondana to Sinhagad.

In the hierarchy of Academy punishments, 'Endurance Hikes to Pt 4311, as Sinhagad is known due to its topographical elevation in feet - is enough to send chills down every cadet's spine. Thoughtful CSMs feel the stone tiles in the sun, and caringly call out the day's temperatures, while reading out the condemned list of winners of said Endurance Hike that weekend.

But does a hike like that dampen a cadet ..? Heck no .. It's supposed to be done from 6:30 AM to 11 AM, and then there's time to get a Liberty card signed and make a trip to Pune, where a buffalo-meat laden King Burger awaits you. You don't question the cheap price, the large serving size, and no one will tell you what animal gave his life to feed your craving for protein.

So with the new Commandant taking charge, fresh regulations mandating Sinhagad hikes as punishments were back in effect. Its effect was almost immediate - Innocents got rousted up, and literally strung, as the need from Sergeant to Squadron Commanders to feed the maw of the monster - as in the headcount showing up at the PT grounds where the run commenced - had to be satisfied.

It was the end of the 5th term, which was tough and unpredictable due to a cross-country shenanigan, that caused a bunch of us a lot of grief (enough said)... Like fledgling eagles (our Squadron), we were raising our heads at the prospect of gaining the privileges of the senior-most term (6th term).

So one fine day, after a class in the ranges or Service areas,which are in the distant hills, physics, and gravity conspired to put us in harm's way, and on our way to a Sinhagad hike. Near the main building (Sudan Block), is the Hut of Rememberance, a lovely place to honour NDA's finest who laid down their lives, and whose names are etched in stone. At the flank of it, is a narrow road, which follows a steep descent, and where, one is forced to 'break formation' of a 2-abreast cycle squad, to a single file, where gravity spurs you on in a welcome breeze through close-cropped hair.

At the base of the said hill, like a coiled Russell's Viper common to the area, hid NCO Ram Niwas Awana, of the RAJPUT Regiment. Awana probably had illusions of superiority, or was not selected as an Officer entry, or frowned on the standard of intake of present lot of cadets - all conspiring to a permanent sneer on his face, and barely concealed contempt. He knew that within 1 year, some of the present lot will be inducted in his Regiment as Officers, in which case he would be compelled to salute them, so he wanted to make the most of the intervening period.

By suddenly popping up in the middle of the narrow road, he ensured mayhem, as 5-6 of us cannon-balled into each other. From there, it was easy pickings, as he gleefully removed our name-tabs, to formally present them for his charge of 'not riding in bike squad' and other sundry violations. Our pleas, despite being blooded and bruised, had little effect on him.

Soon, the bitter fruits of that day presented themselves in the Squadron Order fall -in, where the CSM called out our names, and reminded us of our forthcoming trip to Sinhagad that weekend. It was not just ONE trip, but THREE, ensuring some of us would have to stay back during the term break - to finish the weekly runs - and one of us had a sick parent at home waiting for their son's return.

Cold rage boiled and then distilled into a potent brew. The first week's run was a fiasco. The newbies showed up with all the kit (blankets, mosquito nets etc). I approached the significant weight issue of the pack I would run with, via a 'fresh approach. Out came the scissors and a 2 x 2 ft square of the blanket was cut out. It was stuffed in the backpack in lieu of a proper blanket, that alone weighed 5 kilos.

Since concealment and camouflage classes were where our misery started at the hands of Awana, a small cabin rug, much lighter than a blanket, was packed at the core, and the visible tips were draped over by the blanket piece. Yes, the cadets were asked to show their kit, but only someone twice Awana's sadism would get the blanket extracted for inspection, since it's usually visible anyway. The risk was immense - for sure, one would enter Academy lore. Calls will be made to the Battalion Office, straight from the Adjutant. The officers being ex-NDAs, would privately marvel at such ingenuity, but the heavy hand of discipline will sprinkle even more Endurance Hikes, thereby completing an entire Dante's circle of Hell.

As soon as we were let go at 6:30 AM, barely 100 m away, Awana was there grinning, as he saw his fruits of toxic labor bear sweat. We averted our eyes... As Gabbar Singh told Thakur in 'Sholay' ... 'yaad rakhoonga' (I will remember you), were the words that crossed my mind, and almost slipped out of my mouth.

In the thicket of trees nearby, out came pairs of running shoes, and the heavy ammunition boots that we wore at sendoff, were tied to the backpack, for better mobility.. The thoughtful ones had chosen the right color, mostly black, so as to not be spotted.

As we trundled along in the rising heat, we could see the road had a curiously depressed surface with shiny flecks on it. They had a grim legacy- over the years. From runs past, the surface had been pockmarked, and the horseshoe heels had lost flecks of metal, to make a trail on the asphalt surface ! As the heat picks up, the load, and the sweat ensure your steps become a shuffle instead of a run, and drag your foot on the surface, causing the said 'trail'.

At the base of the hill, some enterprising cadets had set up a deal, one partner would wear the 'lower' portion of a Chindit Order - with belt, ammunition pouches, side pouch and water bottle, while another one would wear the 'upper' - with the heavy blanket, mosquito net and raincape, never mind the season. The 2 would ditch - and hide in the bushes - one half, and climb, suitably lighter. About 50 yards from the summit, they would take the other partner's kit, and be fully kitted up to go, and collect the 'token' - the proof of having completed the run, and then descend to their waiting partner, and do the same in reverse.

En route, misery fell on one of such 'teams'. It had rained a day before, and the 'upper' of one of them had carelessly jettisoned, had slid off into the ravine below ... Horror of horrors, as that meant on the way back, he would be spotted without his gear, and that would be the ticket to more such runs.

Anyway, I completed my trip.. bypassing a cadet in tears, who had not packed a toothbrush among the 45 items or so we are supposed to carry, and all his effort would come to nought. One endurance hike down .. two to go ...

But now, it was time to do some planning. Running in the May heat, and not making it home because of silly charges were not valid options.

Like prisoners, the entire flow of the punishment sequence was analysed with an eye out for weaknesses. We had a very slim chance of success, as 20,000-plus cadets had gone through this, and if they could not find a way to bypass, how could we...? Plus, the penalties of getting caught were surely a loss of 6 months and added training, and endurance hikes.

We started examining the process of this flow of misery, the punishments, looking for any weakness or gap we would exploit. In a nutshell, the punishments for Sinhagarh come from the Academy Adjutant's office in the Sudan Block. They are reported at the Battalion Office level, From there, the names go to the Battalions, and then to Squadron Offices, where, the names are picked up the the CSM, read in the order fall-in, and then passed on to the Drill NCO, to compile the names that would go for that weekend's run.

That means in addition to the Battalion punishment list, there is a SEPARATE piece of paper that shows up 2-3 times a week, ... a paper not much loved .. and so NOT MUCH MISSED at lower levels - that's the Academy-level Punishment Parade state.

Where is the weakness in this ...?

The fact that there is NO central manifest that is tallied. The list is passed down, and not built up. There is no one looking out for it, so if someone could intercept that chain of flow, then something could be done ...? The key was 'how ?'

The CSM has a junior - an understudy, or 'undie' - whose additional job is to pick the Order book, with the stack of papers, and in case the CSM is not needed to show up at the Squadron Office, directly bring the order book to him, or to the Drill Instructor. The said Understudy also often picks the papers from the Battalion Office - the landing place for the Academy-issued punishments. If there was a flaw in the system, where we could arrest our date with Sinhagarh, it was in this triangle between the Squadron Office - Battalion Office and - the Drill Office.

While the CSM's understudy is not to be disturbed, he can't say no to 5th termers, who would be his bosses when the CSM has moved on. Often 5th termers ask to see the Order book, for any surprises, and it was not an unusual ask. One of us would invariably ask for the order book, every day, to scan if our names were there... One fine day, in the cyclostyled list fresh from the Battalion office, we spotted the Academy's punishment parade state - bearing our names and Academy numbers, along with 3x EH printed next to us.

There it lay ... still smelling of the Kores carbon paper ... Like a Greek siren luring sailors to their doom, it beckoned to us. No one had yet seen the list, neither the Squadron office, nor the CSM and certainly not the Drill instructor.

While we were pretending to not notice this vacation-killing death sentence in front of us, we heard the thud of heavy boots ... our fresh, enthusiastic, and intensely gullible Drill NCO was thudding down the polished floors, careful not to slip.

Without a word, we went into synchronised activity. The Understudy was immediately asked to get a bicycle from the bike racks, and sent with a glare, since the CSM was not there to defend him... The Order book was right there, with the day's Routine Orders ... and a rapidly approaching NCO....

There were maybe 5 seconds to act.....

As soon as he stepped off the polished floors which had transfixed his gaze, he would start asking for the days' punishment list. With a rush, a bunch of us greeted him enthusiastically, with a loud 'Ram Ram saab' almost causing him to almost lose his balance. Another one asked him to talk about his exploits while in his previous tenure on the Pak border. I stood ready to ask about his leave plans after the Passing Out parade - a sure tear jerker that would keep him talking animatedly for sure.

With a deft motion, the punishment sheet was detached from the Battalion stack, and like a magician removing a tablecloth underneath a dinner plate, the remaining paper work fell in place - without a mark left in the stapled set. As he was thumbing through the orders, we told him that the Academy Drill Office had called via telephone and had wanted to see him, causing him to not relish the thought of going back before his boss. With the forthcoming Passing Out Parade, there would be tons of berating for him in the near future.

That took care of the situation, as he shuffled off, without any thought for the day's list. Tomorrow, or maybe on another day, a fresh list would arrive, well in time for him to get 3-4 sheets by that weekend, to ensure no one would notice one of the lists was missing.

As the Understudy came back with a bicycle, he was handed over the order book, now without the punishment sheet. Since these sheets were often arriving bunched or with 1-3 days gap, no one knew any better. Orders would be read and the new list would have fresh names for their date with the fortress.

The said group of plotters made their way to lunch, that day's insipid daal-chawal lunch, and the afternoon drill would have no effect on the generally pleasant frame of mind....

Of course it was wrong, and not in the right spirit, but so was the circumstances of our punishment.... So there. If any of us got commissioned into Awana's unit, we would surely have him do Quarter Guard duty, while we would narrate our escape, this time as impetuous 2/Lts

During the term break, the group met at Connaught Place in Delhi over a Nirula's pizza..Out came the now-faded Routing order at a gathering of said colleagues... Someone brought out a lighter, and soon it was a pile of ashes.

No one said a word..

CHAPTER 28 - RUM OR TEA?

After a torrid 5th term in the Academy, including a massive fiasco over X-country which saw relegations, de-tabbing of appointments, debanding of the Cadet Sergeant Major (CSM) and 21-days Restrictions being handed out like candy on Halloween, over the 'suddenly improper' use of hockey sticks on X-country victims post-run, I was badly looking for a change .. on the plus side, those 21 days helped everyone tone up and tighten up, and clear the toe-touch tests before PTI Duni Chand, but then what next to coast over the dreaded Passing Out Parade practice ?

A couple months before the Passing Out Parade, word came from the Squadron office that there was room for 2-3 Army cadets to do a change of service to the Air Force, and that meant a trip to Mysore SSB for a Pilot Aptitude Battery of Tests (PABT). Heat sessions were picking up as every one was in the josh to win or do a good showing at Drill Competition, as till then, we were known as a 'PT Squadron'.

Some months back, suitably pumped by a benign VI term Air Force cadet about 'Air Force being the only manly service' (hmm), I broke the cardinal rule - I volunteered (something which I again did in IMA, with equally disastrous consequences, but that story is for another time).

Eyes turned on me during order fall-in when from the restless pile of authority-defying V-termers on the verge of getting to VI term, I raised my hand.. The CSM told me to put my name up, and I will be notified, in a 'very short time frame'.

Much to my horror, nothing happened as days turned to weeks. Drill competition came and went, and the Battalion Area stone tiles were showing high temperature as the Passing Out Parade drill practices were going through their 'denial-anger-grief' phases of sorrow for one and all involved.

'Cadet Parjan to carry on to Squadron Office' was the announcement as I walked into the Squadron lobby, after a *choley bhatoorey* lunch. 'What the... %^&' as the tingling taste of mango *achaar* gave way to metallic bile rising up.

The Air Force Division Officer smiled like a rose in bloom when he saw me, while the Army Captains there put on a scowl..

Flt Lt : 'Good choice.. now you have to ace the PABT.. Here's your travel warrant .. your trip to Bangalore is booked, but you have to 'travel under your own arrangements' on the way back.'

My heart hit my belly with a thunk.. The passing Out parade was 2 days away.. after that, a trip home to Delhi. All this travel would eat into my leave ! What the heck am I gonna do now.. I had also had the benefit of flying by virtue of Dad being in Indian Airlines, (another fact that caused me much rolling as the seniors caught on to me! wanting to fly while they spent 36 hours travelling on the non air-conditioned NDA special train).

Mournfully, I called home with my little amount of money, and told them of my fate. My evaporating cash position in the STD booth drowned out the tongue-lashing mom was giving me.

Much to my regret later on, I did a half-ass job during the PABT, flunking out on the 'drum test'.. something I could have done better on at any of the SSB-training academies that had popped over by then. Only the thought of getting to Pune, and then by Air to Delhi was on my mind.

In those days, there was a sole train 'Udyan Express' that took a leisurely day in the June heat to get from Bangalore to Pune. My warrant had 'permitted to travel by AC-III tier' stamped in red ink, but the TT did not oblige one bit when I came over hopefully. Me in my walking outs, had to reach him while he was being offered 50-100 Rupee notes (back in 1992) for 'consideration'... money which I did not have, or would not care to give to someone abusing his authority,

Anger begins to build up.... *Kya karein* (what to do ?). The heat in the unreserved coach was unbearable. I was with 2-3 other soldiers, who had been in a similar predicament, but had come to terms with it, and were polishing off an Old Monk with their dinner.

At Dharmawaram or Wadi station, I took the now empty Old Monk, and got to a platform *chaiwallah* ... had him pour some black tea in the bottle, while paying Rs 5 for it ... Another detour to the pantry car for some ice from the cold drink area, and soon the bottle had cooled down. I wrapped it in newspaper, and came back to the TTE.

'Bottle ?' 'Old Monk ?' showing him a quick glimpse of it. He grunted, gesturing me to wait..I was fine with it... I helpfully gave him the gunny bag I had it in, and he motioned me to a berth, which was empty all this while. Much to my relief, he tucked the bottle in his bag, and went on his rounds. I knew he would soon be off duty, and hopefully, won't catch on to the sleight of hand I had carried out. After all, I had promised him a bottle of Old Monk, which was still 'technically true', never mind the contents of the said bottle.

Soon, it was morning, and I had had my sleep, and slipped off to freshen up. At Pune, I took an auto to Lohegaon, then a dusty suburb dominated by the jail, and waited for my flight to Delhi.

I could only imagine the TTE sitting down with some meat/chicken, and a buddy, pouring a drink and the awful truth dawning on him as to what happened here, or with luck, this would be opened after they had had some real booze and then wondering why '*charh kyoon nahin rahee ?*' (why is the rum not hitting).

I am sure he got to settle future transactions with cold hard cash, and not the currency of bottles of Old Monk.

CHAPTER 29 - SIDHU-ISMS

Dec 31 1993 was the day I chose to leave home and join my tank unit as a newly minted 2/Lt. In hindsight, I have always been gullible enough not to leverage the calendar to my advantage or note the significance of dates .. choosing to join NDA Wing Ghorpuri, also on the last day of 1989, while the more enterprising lot chose to make themselves available after celebrating New Years slow dancing away,, and with their hair untouched by the barbers' shears that awaited them...

Back to the date in question ... Dec 31 1993. Having availed the 3 weeks that one gets upon Commissioning, with due warnings about how 'these will be the last free weeks you will enjoy', me and my fellow coursemate booked our short train ride from New Delhi to Nabha. Both of us were commissioned into Armoured Corps, and into units with T-72s, so we felt like cat's whiskers. Our route overlapped, and the coursemate was detraining at Patiala, while I was getting down a couple of stations later at the former princely state of Nabha.

With newly issued fresh bedding holdalls not yet touched by grime, we made ourselves comfortable on the 2 side seats in the AC coach, booked thanks to our freshly issued military warrants.

'Can I sit on the holdall please ..?' a tall smart Sikh gentleman stood in the aisle way, asking us with an earnest smile. Obviously he had spotted an opportunity and the fact that these 2 military guys would be more disposed to accommodating him, than the rest of the AC-dwelling, entitled lot.

The course-mate and I looked at each other, then nodded our heads. In a short while we had lowered our seats, so that the said holdall disappeared, and the gentleman had a seat like the rest of us.

After a while, we could not resist ... he looked VERY familiar, but who was he ..? Could be a former Directing Staff at the academy ?? (Naah, he would order, not ask) , or someone definitely with ties to the uniformed fraternity.

'You look very familiar... Where have I seen you before sir ?' I asked, adding the mandatory 'sir' just in case he was a Captain-saab whom we might run into. The guy looked crestfallen for a minute, adding to my feeling that perhaps he was a gallantry award winner, whom I had inadvertently let down.

'I am Sidhu... Navjot Sidhu' .. he said, looking a bit let down.

No sooner had he said 'Navjot' we jointly blurted 'Sidhu' like small kids ... He looked at us as if we had emerged from under a rock, but then we explained that we never thought a national level cricketer, and future Member of Parliament and media motormouth would grace us - that too without a train reservation. Of course, it was Sidhu, headed back to his family home in Patiala to celebrate the New Year

'*Yaar, last min plan tha.. Intercity pakarni pari*' surmising that the train was the quickest way to get from Delhi to Patiala, rather than battle the traffic on Grand Trunk Road in a taxi.

Soon the rest of the coach was taking turns to meet him, and also bringing casseroles of hot Punjabi lunches, which we too managed to 'hog on'. When the train pulled into Patiala, Siddhu's arrival was greeted like that of a king. Everyone detrained... leaving me watching the sunset at Patiala Cantt, while we waited to move on to Nabha.

Not a bad tale to tell at the New Years Party, I thought to myself.

CHAPTER 30 - 5 ANECDOTES

1. Come...hold it.

In Punjabi, it is common to sound Hindi 'R' as a hard 'dh' e.g. a Tiwari would be called a 'Twadee'. During the mid/late 90s, while on a train journey, I struck a conversation with a Sikh JCO... discussion turned to Music .. This was the time Pakistani singer Nusrat Fateh Ali Khan was hitting the charts with his soulful renderings of qawwalis... and Lisa Ray had shot a great video for 'Afreen Afreen'. (I think it means beautiful or matchless in Urdu)

Naturally I was taken aback, when upon my praising the song, the JCO sported a scowling look and said :

JCO : *Nahin saab, oda gaana nahin changa* (No sir, his songs are not good).

I thought he was criticizing because the singer was Pakistani, so remonstrated that music transcended boundaries etc. and that Fateh Ali had sung many Indian tunes.

JCO ; *Nahin saab, awaaz to theek hai , par oda gaana de bol ne* 'AA FADEEN AA FADEEN' (which in Punjabi is basically urging some one to 'come hold 'it' (referring to a particular part of male anatomy).

For a moment I was speechless, then simply exploded with laughter while the JCO could not fathom what was so funny about such lyrics.

Punjabi is indeed a beautiful language.

2. Z-KITBAG

Once, during my tech innings, I got a pleasant surprise regarding how much interest there is in the processes and techniques used by Armed Forces to get their job done efficiently. I was presenting a session on 'Importance of Communications in the technological age' - a generic, non-exciting topic. After giving an example from the Corporate world on Brainstorming, I switched to 'strategy'... but with a twist.

'Z-KITBAG' is an acronym used to conduct briefings in the Indian Army - from a 3-man trench, to a General-level audience - each letter corresponds to:

- Z for **Zameeni Nishan** (landmarks), or lay of the land.
- K for **Khabar** (Information at hand - about own and enemy disposition)
- I for **Iraada** (Intent)
- T for **Tareeka** (Methodology)
- B for **Bandobast** (Logistics, and administrative arrangements)
- A for **Aapsi Milaap** (Channels of communication, frequencies etc.)
- G for **Ghari Milayen** (Synchronise watches).

It all falls into the acronym of Z-KITBAG that's used by the Army, to brief 18-year old, 10th pass soldiers with rural education, about the task at hand, and the key attributes to share information needed to complete it.

Years later, in a conference room, in far away Silicon Valley, during a snooze heavy day I began going over Z-KITBAG methodology, and interest began to pick up. Jaded Sales people look up from their cellphones .. a few took notes, by the time I get to Bandobast acronym, a couple of very Senior execs are taking notes and pointing animatedly.

Turns out, this simple way resonated to a great degree, and in the break they asked me to document it, and share it at a few other discussions - as in its simplicity, even when applied to the business world, it covered a whole lot of 'gaps' that cause slip-ups in execution - even in a modern, high-tech sales environment.

3. In Pakistan … forever

I was watching the movie 'Emergency' where then Prime Minister, Indira Gandhi mentions to her friend Pupul Jayakar, about her last wishes to not have her ashes immersed in rivers, but to be spread across the Himalayas. I was in the VIII grade, at the time of her demise, and I recalled an Antonov-12 or similar aircraft that had been deployed to cast her ashes over the Himalayas, close to Amarnath cave in Kashmir.

'Glad she would be a part of India' I mused. Then I pulled up Google maps, and began looking for the rivers in that area. The watershed of those mountains drains into Sind river, which drains into Jhelum, which drains into Indus - and flows into Pakistan at Uri.
Her cremated remains were destined to flow into Pakistan !

So there is a good chance that along with the rumored gold deposits that flowed into Pak via Himalayan rivers, are the ashes of the Indian PM who dismembered them during the 1971 War.

While Jinnah's house in Mumbai will never be a part of Pakistan, Indira will continue to be a part of their ecosystem - forever.

4. Saved by a thunderstorm

My love for all things military continued unabated, even after I bid adieu and headed to the civilian side of life. The movie 'Border' was having its first showing that day, a Friday the 13th (Jun, 1997). It was a much awaited movie with a stellar cast of who's who of 90s era Bollywood. It featured an iconic poster of Sunny Deol holding a 84 mm Carl Gustav rocket launcher and was based on the 1971 Indo-Pak war's battle of Longewala.

The day had started badly for me as my scooter had skidded on a loose pile of red sand (*Badarpur*), leading to a couple of stitches - thankfully NOT on my squash racket hand.

I had a new job, and used to carry my squash racket for a post-job game at Siri Fort Sports Complex, much to the amusement of civilian co-workers. That day, I wrapped up a post-lunch meeting in Vasant Vihar, but still got delayed getting to the movie hall, due to thunderstorms delaying me. By the time I got there, I saw a massive crush of people trying to get in. All hell was breaking loose.

There was no way I could go in, that too with a squash racket in hand. I thought of dropping it at a Xerox shop I frequented, and getting in the scrum.

And then, a couple of raindrops fell, and a *aandhi* (dust squall) blew in. The furnace-like heat of June in Delhi cooled noticeably, as I fiddled with my racket.

Realizing it would be tough to buy - or pay double the price for the tickets from the touts - I decided to head to the squash courts to play in the cooler weather. Ran a few rounds, swam a few lengths and played a couple of games.

Distant sirens sounded, but since India's leading hospital AIIMS was nearby, I did not think twice. When I got out, there was panic and chaos all around. To everyone's horror, the movie hall, *Uphaar* had gone up in flames due to a short circuit caused by negligent fire security measures, spawning a fire that killed 59.

Had it not been a thunderstorm, and had I managed to get a ticket, I would have been in the balcony, where the most fatalities happened. The management had locked the doors from outside, and added unauthorised seating to maximize ticket sales.

A thunderstorm, and a love of squash from my Army days, saved my life.

5. Bikaneri feasts

If there ever was a foodie town in North West India, it would be Bikaner, in historical Rajasthan state. . When we were deployed in the dusty spring of 1994 along Bikaner-Lun Karansar axis, during Corps-level 'Exercise Bhavani Khadka' (Goddess's Sword), a trip to the city would be eagerly awaited. Between the exercise phases, the much welcomed 'lull in battle' would have us youngsters beseech the Captains, to 'take us with them.'

An open-top Jonga from the recce troop would be commandeered, and we would clamber on. *Putkas* (headgear) flying, we would press on the deserted highway, scaring the *neelgais* and black bucks along the way.

In those pre-cellphone era days, long distance calls were costly. The goal was to be there at the phone booth by 9 PM, when the STD (Subscriber Trunk Dialing ... not the other medical acronym) pulse would drop to 25% rate for our weekly call home.

Reaching Bikaner around sunset at 7, we would dig into the munchies - *namkeen* and *rasgulla/gulab jamuns*. A good quantity would be ordered for our troops and parcelled.

On the way back, we would stop at a *dhaba* eatery and feast on Rajasthani cuisine - *laal maas* (red fiery chili mutton curry), *kair sangri* (vegetarian dish made from berries) and *gopal gattas* (kofta like dish), washed down with Old Monk rum and warmish water from the leather '*chaagal*', and of course, namkeen...

The area has a proud martial tradition, and often they would not charge, but we were adamant on paying. An officer always pays his dues in a professional army.

CHAPTER 31 - TARGET STOPPED ... 125 GUN CLEAR !

An Account of my 1st Tank firing

The Indian Army has a tradition – the Officers visit the Junior Commissioned Officers (JCOs) (equivalent to Staff Sergeants and higher than NCOs– the soldiers' leaders) at their Mess on India's Independence Day (Aug 15) , and the JCOs return the visit to the Officers Mess on the Republic Day (Jan 26), to socialize over drinks.

Thanks to the colder weather in Jan, the JCOs' propensity to imbibe beer is a bit subdued than if they were to visit in Aug – so the Mess liquor's sanctity and overall quantity are preserved..

So here I was in Nabha, Punjab - 26 days into my unit, barely beginning to learn the ins and outs of a T-72 tank, and getting to know things.. There was plenty to keep me busy as is -

- Being robustly sent on round-the-clock guard checks (ensuring sentries are up at 2 AM in foggy Punjab plains),
- expected to be the next Cross-country runner to follow in my Academy-medallist predecessor,
- expected to play an 'Officer sport' like Squash, and
- pass the feared regimental Silver test on our haloed history and the story behind every battle honor and former accounts of valor.

In short, I had enough activities to keep a 'youngster' on toes with barely any time to attend my garage lessons or 'pre-course', leaving our Training *Daffadar* (Sargeant) Dharam Singh disappointed.

'*Saab, kab aaoge garage main ..?*' (Sir, when will you show up for lessons in the garage ?') he would bemoan in a sad voice, to which I had no answer.

Soon it was 26 Jan, and right after the CO's *Darbaar* (Assembly), we got to the Officers Mess, to await the JCOs - trays of steaming hot '*kaleji*' (liver) lined up in welcome for the aficionados known to hijack the choicest cuts of mutton to their kitchens.

In walked the Unit adjutant and read aloud a message :

'63rd Cavalry is doing field firing at Mahajan ranges and needs Officer-observers' as he cast a baleful eye at me, probably sad at having me go unhindered for a few days.

'So much for drinking the JCOs under the table' ... I thought, relishing the prospect of being out a bit and stretching my legs.

The beer tankards were quickly drained, crumbs of 'egg-on-toast' brushed off, and a jeep arrived with Maj Sharma, my benign mentor attached to our unit from Infantry, 'Chandy-sir' our 'Alpha' Squadron Commander and myself, and the driver. The majors took over the wheel themselves, leaving nothing for me and the driver to do, while sitting in the back and perpendicular to the direction of motion on the highway. Off we headed on the day-long drive into the desert towards Mahajan Field Firing Ranges (MFFR) from southern Punjab via Bhatinda, Pili Banga, Suratgarh.

The next morning, we were up bright and early at the range. The then General Officer Commanding (GOC) of 1st Armoured Division (Black Elephant), was Gen Shamsher 'Shammi' Mehta – a reputed and formidable leader - befitting the commander of India's oldest and most prestigious strike formation responsible for taking the battle across its western borders. 63rd Cavalry was his unit, and his son was our Battalion Under Officer who had been commissioned into the unit 6 months back, so had known about them a bit as they had put up a firepower demonstration in the last months of our Academy training.

I had expected to be an observer sitting in an elevated tent a few 100 yards away from the firing point. I had barely started learning about the tank, and 3 weeks is just about right for you to get yourself killed in a few dozen myriad ways by a steel behemoth, attributable to me doing something careless or stupid.

By noon, it was hot and dusty, as columns of fine Rajasthan desert dust churned upwards, as the tanks carried out regular runs firing, lining up on simulated start lines and assaulting and discharging 125 mm rounds with their 2A46GSP smooth bore main guns.

I was asked to 'hop aboard' a tank ready to fire... they were firing on the move, in fully automatic mode. That means the gun turret was not being moved manually, but electrically, and it can move real fast - as quickly as a stick waved in air. This is called a 'stabilized shoot' as the main 125 mm gun is stabilized by the fire control system as the tank bumps along the desert terrain, with the aiming mark squarely set on the target.

On Youtube, there is a video of a German tank with a large beer tankard perched on top of its barrel's business end, filled to the brim, but barely spilling a drop - that's how the stabilizer works in a tank, as it lays the aiming mark squarely on the target and corrects itself as the tank is driven at combat speed.

I perched myself on one of the smoke grenade dischargers, as the tank roared off on a 2 km run. Older British designed Vijayanta and ex-Soviet T-55 tanks, referred to as derelicts were being used as targets. Some of the soldiers had fought the 1971 War in those very tanks, and were not too thrilled about seeing their 'life savers' now being used for target practice. The troops are fervently attached to their weapons platforms and it shows.

I was trying to reach across to the gunner to let me know when he fires so I don't fall off the tank, but as expected, over the radio chatter and the general focus on the prevailing environment, he had better things to take care of than a green behind-the-ears young officer from another unit, and so I could not reach to him. I sat royally ignored and unable to follow the fast paced events unfolding around me.

Suddenly, I saw the main barrel recoil, a 'loud whoosh' as an orange tongue of flame spat out, and with a jaw-knocking recoil, a 10-kg projectile launched, with its enclosing sabot (case that encloses a round through its journey in the barrel) dropping to the ground a few 100 yards away … the tank had hit the derelict.You are supposed to keep your mouth open, else the shock wave can knock your teeth , but I had no time to remember that.

I thought maybe that's it, and now that the round was fired, we would head back to the cool embrace of the Officers Mess tent, and have a beer or two - but that was not to happen.

The R-123 radio set crackled to life, and everyone hearing it stiffened. The tank stopped abruptly, and out of nowhere Chandy-sir came on board . He relayed word that Gen Mehta had arrived at the firing range's Control tower and everyone better get into full-blown battle mode ASAP.

He took on the radio headset and spoke a series of "Yes sir's" and ending with another 'Yes sir, the youngster is fine and wants to fire'. Hanging up, and then smiling back at me.

Here I was, less than a month in service, with hardly 10 hours of tank training, barely knowing enough to fire a tank except a few instructions, now being expected to fire live rounds, without any simulator experience– that too on a tank of another regiment, with the formation commander witnessing it firsthand, from the Mobile Control Tower (MCT) most likely, which still was very close indeed.

How close?, I was about to find out.

A few minutes later, only the driver was left with the tank, as the gunner and the JCO from 63 Cav too dismounted and walked away towards the rear. Meanwhile, unknown to me, in the heat, the 'Gun ready to fire' light was not coming on when the gunner, muttering under his breath - bailed on me… obviously, the tank can't fire till the light comes on in the instrument panel.

A Maruti Gypsy with a flashing red beacon pulled up next to the tank, and stopped, disgorging its passengers. One look and the feeling 'I am doomed' washed over me. Out stepped a tall strapping Sikh Brigadier – Brigadier CS Harika, our Brigade Commander - an otherwise paternal, father-figure who would hold forth long talks on ethos and tradition, but at this moment he looked like he would rather not have his boys make a fool of themselves before his boss, the GOC himself.

I silently wished for Maj Sharma to be around for some courage and inspiration – 'He's probably in the Officers Mess tent by now' I thought gloomily … Chandy-sir gave up his place on the tank to Brig Harika – and in the Commander's cupola/seat slid in a stylishly camouflage attired figure, with the crossed sword and baton insignia on his shoulders– the GOC himself.

I was now in the gunner seat...that's about 12 inches shoulder-to-shoulder space in the cramped confines with the roar of the diesel engine, the clanging of gears and the chatter over the multiple radio sets in operation.

The tank was seriously pulling rank now with a Maj Gen, a Brigadier, a decorated Major with Sena Medal (Gallantry) award and a single-star 2nd Lieutenant (me) - it was a miracle so much brass was not bogging it down in the Rajasthan sand... probably my lightness in the hierarchy was keeping us from getting sucked in.

'Walk me through what you see, youngster ! .. and why are you not firing in stab shoot mode ?' – said the GOC, all the while talking to at least 3 persons at once, including over 2 radio sets.

I went over the landmarks, the designated target.. this was no longer briefing your Academy Platoon Commander about the field of fire from a 3-man LMG trench. The battle camouflage on the tanks was real, so was the sound of diesel sloshing around in a round carousel below our feet, with tank ammo and rounds loaded in it .. a constant reminder of how quickly we could be wiped off the face of the earth, due to any error... felt like sitting in death's lap itself, should it all go up - as it does, once a while..

My heart drained faster than the fluid in a tank's transfer case when both its driving sticks were pulled back to a complete stop.

'Sir, I am ready to proceed' hoping that I recalled enough of the process to not make a fool of myself but with the same confidence as one tells your Academy superiors that your room has 'always been ready' for inspection, no matter how messed up it is behind the door.

Meanwhile, the gun still wouldn't be ready in the firing position, as it would not come to the projectile loading angle ... it's needed to be there so a thick chain, called the rammer chain launches from behind like a furious cobra, hits the round lined up to load into the barrel, and pushes the round and it's ammo in the main gun... this is no bicycle chain.. nearly 2 inches thick, it launches fast like a nun-chuck, quick enough to easily decapitate and load in the main gun's yawning dark breech block, the head of anyone foolish enough to peek in the barrel, while the chain is unleashed behind him... Imagine dying like that, in your own tank, and not while doing something heroic.

I went over the firing procedure.

'All Circuit Breakers 'ON' as we both flipped the 10 circuit breakers each on Gunner and Commander side

'ABT switch on 'Ruch' (Mode of operation switch for auto loader based firing)

'Magazine on Load'

'Cassette up' (mechanism that helps load and unload in automatic mode)

Miraculously, I could see the 'Blue light on- gun ready to fire light finally come back on.The resetting of the circuit breakers had cleared the finicky mechanism and the blue light came on after what seemed like eternity.

I let the Laser range finder shoot a laser beam to the target and got the range.

'Shell ranging 800 .. traversing left' meaning we would be firing an Armor piercing round at 800 m.

I pressed my forehead hard and kept gazing through the 67 kg sight-cum-range finder, TPD-K1, as the greenish glow of the viewfinder came around me... lining up the aiming mark on the hapless derelict tank a km away, I continued

' ON !'

The gun cradle was whirring and the servo motors underneath engaged, adjusting and keeping the main gun on the target as we went over the sand dunes.

'Fire' came the reply from the GOC.

'Firing now', I yelled as I pressed the electrical firing switch with my forefinger on the joystick. The gun boomed in the enclosed space, as 10 kg of charger lit up. The auto-loader whirred, the spent shell popped out of the barrel, caught by the catcher with a frame, and then ejected via a quickly opening door activated by a servo motor.

Those Russian Ivans are nifty designing such a perfect killing machine, or so I thought.

All this took place in about 10 seconds, as a good crew can fire off 3 aimed rounds of tank ammo in under a minute, when well trained...

The round I had fired punched a hole through the armor of the target, leading to sparks and molten metal for a few seconds in a dying cascade of yellow-orange embers. Everyone cheered.

'Target stopped, 125 gun clear'

'125 gun clear', I replied, as I ensured the main gun was free of any rounds.

The auto-loader whirred again, the main gun came back to the projectile loading angle, up came another APFSDS round from the magazine, with its black-grey Tungsten Carbide penetrator glistening in the dome light...

The rammer chain pushed the APFSDS into the barrel, retracted, the gun went to charger loading angle, a 10 kg propeller charge came up, duly hit by the rammer and the breech block slammed shut..

I was beginning to enjoy myself .. but then things changed for the unexpected again.

'Youngster, let's now fire in manual mode !' .. said the GOC, intent on maximizing my near vertical learning curve, while calling out to the driver to stop. Brig Harika peeked over from my side... sternly and silently urging me to not screw up now. Miraculously, he, Chandy sir and others were hanging on to the outside of the tank, while I was aiming and moving the gun in auto mode..

But it was here that I was most vulnerable ..

I had, in the unit garage, only learnt about the automatic firing option – it is glamorous, more like a video game. But the manual firing is a different beast, calling for more skill in aiming and is done with a different trigger, one that I had only looked at somewhere between my knees, as I was more interested in auto-mode firing. I felt a bit like 'Abhimanyu' from the Mahabharata, who had learnt how to enter a circular battle formation called 'Chakra Vyuh' - but not learnt how to exit from it.

I put my hand on the manual rotating handle that elevates or depresses the main gun ... the manual trigger is somewhere 'down there', but there is a metal flap that covers it, sort of like a nuclear weapon's trigger in Bond movies, and that flap needs to be lifted to access the trigger, for safety reasons.

I did not know that yet... I started the loading process, saw the breech block slam shut, and the blue light came on again.

'Fire when ready' said the GOC. I began pressing on the flap trying to feel the trigger.

No result. Pressed again, no result..

'Um... yes sir' I mumbled...clammy fingers still searching. I was worried that I would accidentally fire while the gun was away from the target, and while not killing anyone on the range, would shoot it so off the mark that it would be a joke for decades.

My thumbnail managed to lift the flap, and I could see the button's outline... Just as the GOC began to turn to me with a puzzled look as to what was holding me up – I pressed hard and fired ..The round hit the target smack between the turret and the chassis, separating the turret, which went flying upwards like a coin when tossed by a flick of the thumb...

'Nice shot' or words to that effect were said by the GOC, as I breathed a sigh of relief ... In a space of 10 minutes, it was all over.

We turned the tank around. Word had spread among the 63 Cavalry troopers that another unit's young officer had fired their tank, and the tradition dictates the men be given signed slips of sweets and rum as a 'thank you'. I signed off on a few slips that day .... probably most of my pay for that month went into Old Monk.

I staggered into the Officers mess, suddenly parched.. I had politely declined their CO, Col. Gill's offer for a beer earlier in the day, but now I was so thirsty, I was chugging down the beer mug, just as Col Gill walked in complaining to Maj Sharma ' He doesn't drink or what...?'.

Their eyes widened at the sight of me downing a beer all the way.

I thanked him again, and was called and thumped on the back by the GOC.Soon he was gone in a flurry of salutes as over a 100 messages and situation reports awaited his attention... Everyone breathed easier.

6 months later, in Aug, at the KK ranges in Maharashtra, I was at a different range.. not a desert but a calm, monsoon like ambiance of a training ground. For the first time firers in our batch, points are deducted if they were to miss the 30 second window in which to engage and fire, and they would be roundly cursed for that by the Captain Instructor, as that would mean the tank would need to be stopped or brought back, but in my case, both rounds found the mark even before the first turn ...

It was not like it was my first time ... was it ?

CHAPTER 32 : EK THA TIGER (Once, there was a tiger)

It would be a cliche to say that someone you barely met, off-and-on, over a 11 months intense training period - yet still claim to have a bond forged in fire .. except when it really IS forged in fire.

And not just any fire - the muzzle and backblast from the formidable 84 mm Carl Gustav rocket launcher -referred to as the 'Battalion Commander's Artillery'.

Sunny Deol's 'Border' movie weapon. A rocket launcher par excellence.

That was my connection with Col. Satnam 'Tiger' Bajwa - forged way back when we were wrapping up our training at the Indian Military Academy (IMA) in Dehradun.

While the moniker of a tiger is given to any officer with a pulse who can twirl a mustache- his was given to him apparently by those he hunted - the Pakistan-Afghan origin terrorists inducted in the cauldron of Kashmir of the 1990s. That time, they had better Chinese grenades, weaponry, and body armor, compared to us. Yet, he took them on - in raids, ambushes across multiple cordon-and-search operations that marked a typical day in 90s era Kashmir.

From verbal duels over the radio in chaste Punjabi outlining their dubious pedigree, to having an impressive (read lethal) combat record, Bajwa ruled the roost.

He owned his Area of Responsibility (AoR), causing militancy to retreat, at a time when Liberated zones were popping up and India on the back foot taking on a belligerent Pakistan.

To get him, they laid an elaborate ambush using a land mine (yup.. nasty way to go upstairs), but he survived that, with a foot injury that caused him to ultimately change his arm from the JAT Regiment to the Army Ordnance Corps (AOC).

Not easy to put such a guy down.

That day during our final term in the Academy at Dehradun, we had Rocket Launcher firing at the Academy a month before commissioning. In hindsight, we were adrenaline junkies, chasing thrills such as racing up the 10 m board to jump in the pool.. and that day a chance presented itself.

While some shy away from that fearsome weapon due to the intense blast and ear pain it causes when one fires the allotted 2 rounds. Many choose to press the trigger, unmindful of the aim, and just being glad to be done with it.

By contrast, we were just happy pressing the trigger when our turn came. After we were done firing, the NCO announced that a few extra rounds had been unpacked and needed to be fired, as they couldn't be stored in a safe way after being uncrated, with the fuses primed and made ready for the firing..

Sensing silence, The Weapons Training Officer berated the rest of the batch for laziness, while my and Bajwa's hands shot up- initially ignored, but then we were called up.

Round after round we fired - peering down its pendulum sight- our faces caked in glee and dust. The backblast blew up clouds of dust, covering the firing position for minutes, and the WTO himself gasping for air. We must have fired at least a dozen rounds each, versus the stipulated 2 rounds the training mandated.

Our hearing was gone for 2-3 days, but who cared.

One recent evening, after he settled into a security role with a large MNC, Tiger was sipping his favorite drink.. perhaps God wanted someone to sort out the trouble makers .. or may be there were a few RL rounds available in heaven... along with his drink.. and so his call came

RIP Bajwe.. ek tha tiger .. woh hai tu.

A brave son of India

... a dear friend.

CHAPTER 33 : KHOONI DARWAAZA (Bloody Gate)

On a busy road known as the Fleet Street of Delhi, took place a custodial triple execution that changed the course of Indian history; ended the Mughal dynasty ; and cemented the British grip on the Indian subcontinent for almost a century, eventually leading to its Partition, and its eternal bitterness to this day.

On a day during my visit back home, I resolved to make a trip to that location.

I had been meaning to make this particular trip since I was a 2/Lt, in 1993, just commissioned into one of the most traditional tank units, when I came to know of this event. The unit was born in the tempest of the Revolt of 1857 (aka the Sepoy Mutiny per the British, and the First War of Indian Independence by Indian historians).

Few events were as transformational as the Indian Sepoy Mutiny that raged from May 1857 till spring of 1858 - that led to establishment of British rule in India from 1857 to 1947 when India finally gained independence.

Tens of thousands would die- be it in the freedom struggle,.... in the World War arenas of Flanders and Cassino and El Alamein.. in droughts such as the Bengal Famine and in the Partition blood-letting.

Few events were more key than the Siege (and Relief) of Delhi at that time, and within that.... the killing of the princes of the last Mughal emperor by an English Captain, in an act that would be considered cold-blooded murder and a war-crime today.

But first a bit of history....

In the mid 1800s, the Great Game of denial of warm water ports on the Arabian sea to the Russian Czars was in its early but definitive stages. The British looked at the stretch between Kabul and Delhi through the prism of multiple invasions that came down Khyber Pass, right from Alexander's times. Any invader breaking through, would meet with a force sent out by Delhi, and battle it out in towns like Panipat (3 wars) and Tarain.

Come 1857, and unrest in the British Indian Army was at its peak.The sepoys mutinied over the use of beef/pork greased cartridges introduced by the British for use in the new Lee Enfield rifles. Ignoring religious taboos, the procedure to load the rifle required the soldiers to bite into the tallow coated cartridges, violating the core religious beliefs on beef for Hindus and pork for Muslims, on account of them being perceived as unclean.

The flames or rebellion, fanned by pay and other grievances within the British Indian army, which was led by British officers, but manned with Indian soldiers spread fast and wide - the spirit of revolt or 'ghadar' was fanned , leading them to attack and overpower their officers, and charge to Delhi, to implore the last Mughal emperor in the Red Fort, Bahadur Shah Zafar, to take over the reigns and free them of the curse of the 'fi-rangi' (literal meaning 'without colour'). From Barrackpore, to Merrut, to Peshawar to Vellore, no part of India was safe for the British in a matter of days.

Despite a strong presence in Delhi, the British were taken aback, as the rebellion took on a religious 'us versus them' colour, and with Delhi being a predominantly Muslim city then, was full of religious ghazis, jiyalas and followers of puritanical Islam, who saw this as a chance to re-raise the 'Nizam-e-Mustafa' under the Mughal banner.

Outrages were committed, including looting and murder, of defenceless European civilians, including women and children, with prince Mirza Khizr, at the forefront of such acts.Similar acts of violence, sieges in places like Delhi's Red Fort and Fatehgarh, lead to a firming of British resolve to pay back. The same would occur at Kanpur and Lucknow, and would become a rallying cry to avenge the dead who perished in the service of the Crown.

In their desperation, they turned to their erstwhile opponents - the so-called 'Martial races' of Sikhs, Pathans and Gurkhas - who saw it fit to help an alien power re-establish its writ, then choose to align with their countrymen in overthrowing them. Historical grudges and divisions were to be blamed for such an outcome.

Various horse columns or 'Irregular Horse' were formed to come to the relief of Delhi, which had been taken over by the rebels, and the Mughal Emperor back in charge... and they rode non-stop.

These soldiers did not disappoint. Tough hardy frontiermen and avid horsemen who lived their lives in the saddle, soon were swooping down the Grand Trunk Road, indulging in skirmishes with the erstwhile Bengal Army deserters and mutineers in Kunjpura and Badli, till they ran into the rebel fortifications on the Northern ramparts of Kashmiri Gate, at Qudasia Bagh, a garden now known for its pitched battles.

One of those who raised a horse column was Capt William Hodson, who led a column - Hodson's Horse - of Sikhs and Pathans, traditional enemies, who were content to serve under the fair regime of the Englishman. Herein lies the reason as to why the British ruled over so many .... while being so few themselves.

Around 22 Sep, Major Hodson deposed and took into custody the doddering Mughal Emperor, who had hid at the tomb of the Emperor and his ancestor, Humayun. Unlike Humayun, who underwent untold hardships, Zafar had a reluctance to battle it out. Seeking assurances of his safety, he was imprisoned in the Red Fort itself, while being considered for execution.

Hodson rousted the Mughal contingent,, along with 2 of his sons and grandsons, and with utter calm held off the 100s who had surrounded his small mounted contingent, as they made their way back to the City..

The Delhi of that time began and ended at the fortress walls of the Red Fort. The stretch outside Delhi Gate, till Humayun Tomb was deserted, as it was between the earlier Afghan settlement, and the newer Mughal dynasty. And it was here that the arch stood, not serving any real purpose, with a sinister name - *Khooni Darwaaza* (Bloody Gate).

Like London's Traitors Gate, this arch was destined for infamy. 2 sons of a prior nobleman had their heads displayed here in the centuries past, when they conspired against the Crown Prince Jehangir, romantically portrayed as prince Khurram of Anarkali's love story, but a malevolent violent opium-addicted character himself. 2 generations later, as Dara Shikoh lost the battle of succession, to his sibling Aurangzeb, his head too was displayed here. So were bodies of assorted killers and executed criminals.

On 22nd Sep, as the Emperor and his princes were sent back to the Red Fort in captivity, they, and their British captors, were soon surrounded by a growing mob, 'as far as the eye could see' per Hodson, and many dressed as 'Ghazis' with white shrouds tied to their heads, indicating a readiness to die in battle. Soon darkness would fall, and with that, the chances of the British to take their prisoners to the safety of the Fort.

This is where it gets unclear... Did Hodson carry a desire for vengeance for the deaths of women and children at the behest of Mirza Khizr and Prince Abu Bakr ? Did he see this as a way to end the ever present Sword of Damocles of Mughal succession, once and for all ?

Or was he, deeply scared, yet displaying immense courage, carrying out an act of utmost cold-bloodedness that would have the natives scurrying for cover, and in turn protect him through his display of violence?

Upon reaching Khooni Darwaaza, Hodson rode at the head of the column, and had the Mughal princess dismount and get in the arched structure. There, he had them undress, and used his Victoria carbine to shoot them one by one, in an act of ultimate ignominy. Their bloody corpses were then loaded back, and with the natives watching, dumped into the Kotwaali (police station) near Red Fort - the spot from where the princes' outrages had begun.

Karma would soon catch up. The next summer (1858) - after chasing the rebels from Delhi to Lucknow - Hodson would run into a fatal volley deep in the defence of the Lucknow Residency and die proclaiming 'I hope I did my duty'.

The Mughal emperor would die in exile in Rangoon in Burma, and the East India Company Flag would soon give way to the British Flag, after the post-1857 consolidation of the Company into the British Empire. Come 1994, a slender 2/Lt would pose in front of a canvas print of Maj Hodson, and his carbine, visualising and planning a visit 'soon'. It only took 27 years for it to happen.

The Arch is now hidden in the median, of a road named after the Mughal emperor Bahadur Shah Zafar. It seems to be shrouded in trees, unlike other gates of Delhi that have wide open access.

Perhaps it is hiding from its own history. No one knows.

CHAPTER 34 - PODIUM FINISHES

'Kuch kariye.. kuch kariye... " (Let's do something !) so the song of the sports movie 'Chak De India' goes - Shahrukh's magnum opus on Hockey. But a medal has come to hockey's natural home after 41 years. - . A nation that won back-to-back Olympic Golds for 8 straight Olympics from 1928 to 1984... suddenly found itself on the outside once the grass courts were changed to Astro turf, and stamina became key over skill.

India, the land of hockey wizard Dhyan Chand, who was offered a Colonel's rank by Hitler himself in '36 Berlin Olympics... a wizard whose hockey stick was broken up to check if he had a secret magnet; so great was his control of the ball - was, for decades denied a podium finish, let alone a hockey gold.

At a time when the cricket world's superstars from UK, Aus and NZ were still turning their noses up at touring India - so unlike now when they are here all year round, looking ridiculous wearing suits while standing on a 45 C hot day, it was hockey - without the need to have 'field' prefixed to it, that had the common man socialist appeal of soccer, that won the hearts of a Nehruvian India.

As a 8 year old, when India won Olympic Gold for the last time in the West-boycotted Moscow Olympics of 1980, I went to our landlord's home for a function to honor a crown prince of hockey - Mohammad Shahid, whose attacks as a left-out paired with Zafar Iqbal, were a sensation. Shahid grew up a stones' throw away, and our landlord was a rich brick kiln owner. Shahid showed up surrounded by a mob, ill at ease with a sports blazer, and carrying a foot high 'Misha' bear doll from Moscow.

It was an Indian team like no other - with Catholic tribals like Dung Dung and the ever-present Sikhs in the form of Gurmail and Surinder Sodhi, and names like Thoiba Singh and Joaquim Carvalho... a microcosm of India itself, where the stylism of UP players from aristocratic landed class like KD Singh Babu and Salim Sherwani was giving way to the soon to arrive generation of Dhanraj Pillay and other players from all over India.

London's Prudential Cup success of 1983 was still 3 years away, a win at Lords stadium on a July day which would bring cricket on the ascendant, and cause hockey to subtly recede from the national imagination. During the 80s, India's talent pool often played barefoot on scrub, and there were probably 3 astroturfs in the entire nation. J

Just keeping that turf wet was a challenge. Nations like South Korea, Spain and Holland and Germany ruled a hockey field where the eternal flourishes and stickwork of the sub-continent gave way to brute force hits launched from D to D.

As we butted heads with eternal enemy Pakistan in both cricket and hockey, we respected their immense talent pool in both sports. Our admiration and jealousy of our neighbor - be it players like Hassan Sardar in Hockey or Imran Khan in Cricket - only had us aspiring for a pre-partition united team playing and defeating the rest of the world.

But what we lacked in mental and physical toughness, we made up for in enthusiasm... and after decades, the wheel would turn , and give India medal podium finishes at Olympics.

Personally, in NDA, I played in 3rd string hockey, a level known for physicality or playing rough, rather than much skill, with '*ek do teen chaar.. goal nahin to dhakka maar*' (if you cant score a goal then play rough) being our mantra to take down anyone coming close to my scythe like hockey sweep as a half-back. The same lack of technique almost cost me my eye when I was playing 6-a-side hockey within the unit, being at an off-side violation to a blow I did not stop in time.

Like all Banarasis, Shahid was enamored of the city he grew up in - his desire to not leave the eternal city meant he gave up much more lucrative opportunities upon retirement, and declined to move to the money and power centers of Delhi or Mumbai, instead content with a mid-level job with the Railways, and untimely passing away of complications due to jaundice.

Shahid would be proud of Team India today. We finally regained our podium finishes.

Chak ditta India ! (We did it India !)

CHAPTER 35 - SHAMMING THE MAST

A tribute to dear Jagbir S Kataria, a proud brother-in-arms)

Mid-Nov 1990

The lobby of the Science Block at NDA looked like a walking-wounded aid post and the naval Petty Officer, himself a Jat from Bhiwani, looked disapprovingly at the handful of cadets who had been told to report to him. All were 2nd termers, the lucky ones wearing club attire, and the ones who came from tough squadrons like Echo or Charlie, came straight from a Battalion area session, with the dirt clinging on to their sweat soaked, olive-green jerseys.

The evening before, as if on cue, the outgoing CSMs had turned and looked at the 2nd termers, instead of talking through the 3rd termers, and like a prison doctor making selections, told 2-3 of us to go to the Science Block the next day for 'shamming the mast'. 'Lucky buggers', we heard him mutter.

The correct term is 'manning the mast' but if you are not sweating it out on the parade ground (due to either punishment commitments, or being on a warning list for any reason), then it was deemed 'shamming' (taking it easy).

The pride of place at the parade ground, and as a depiction of the triservices nature of training - is the Quarter Deck and the 99-ft tall mast of a British light cruiser, HMS Ajax, which fought the German battleship, Graf Spee in the Battle of River Plate off Montevideo, Uruguay.

The ship was later sold to the Indian Navy, and was reborn as INS Delhi. Upon retirement from service, its mast was positioned at the quarter deck of the parade ground.

Of course, INS Delhi name was reborn, and now adorns a Made-in-India battleship much more capable than her predecessor. As the outgoing course slow-marches to 'Auld Lang Syne' and salutes the quarter deck, about 2 dozen juniormost course cadets climb the rope rigging on the mast, and cheers them on..... that's the plot, and the reason for us mustering that day.

Military training does not simply displace fear inside our minds, through lectures or classes on how to combat our innermost demons. There is no pill to take to become fearless in one go. It is done by displacing it out, and replacing it by a stronger force.

As the Petty officer brought our herd to the quarterdeck for the first time, we felt as a group we were doomed. The ropes led up to a yardarm halfway up the mast. As we were lined up as per size, the puny ones, myself included, found ourselves set to climb to the highest parts of the mast.

The steel rope at the core was cold, and years of glossy white paint on the wooden yardarm had made it slippery under our flimsy PT shoes. Wind would buffet the entire structure, as it would creak under our collective exertion, sending waves of panic as we learnt to climb it speedily, without missing a step.

As luck would have it, the yardarm and the crows nest up top - became happy perches for fellow non-techies. Randhawa took the crows' nest, and myself, Jagbir and Saharan spread out on the yardarm, with a slim metal cable to hold behind our back.

The drill was that as the slow march began of the Senior squadron, us juniors would run through the rows of parents and dignitaries in a single file - in vests, cummerbunds and white trousers, and within 30 seconds, climb up the nets. So while every cadet in the Academy looks up at the mast, we would have a birds' eye view and look down at the entire assembled parade - all 1,020 souls.

But this was not the end of the maneuver.

There is a flypast by the Air Force. Then recently inducted MiG29s, accompanied by Jaguars from nearby Pune's Lohegaon air force base would come screaming across - and directly in the faces of those of us perched precariously on the mast, to the point where one could see the faces of the pilot.

The sound wave felt like a physical force pushing us backwards, into thin air, as a fine mist of burnt aviation fuel descended around us. A net was there to arrest the fall of anyone losing his footing or grip, lest their fall cause injuries to the VVIP dignitary underneath. Even so,falling from that height would give such whiplash, that chances of getting hurt were just as bad as splaying on the quarterdeck without any protection.

As timing to execute this had to be precise, the culling of those unable to hold on or being fidgety or fearful had begun. One day we found Jagbir, engrossed in a conversation with one of the enthusiastic, but fidgety cadets, who, after being coaxed and motivated in turn, shaped up pretty well and managed to hold on to his spot in the lineup. Jagbir and I would be on the yardarm, gripping the cable and muttering jokes under our breath.

And so the day arrived.... As the appointments took place in the senior squadron, we arrived en masse to cries of 'Dad ...look here' from the rows of parents and siblings seated at the parade ground. Feet rising in sync, chest high, and a mass of media photographers around the quarter deck, we launched ourselves at the mast, one last time. Our next meeting with the quarter deck would be 2.5 years later, when we would step under it and salute it in slow march.

Lazily, the glint of the fighters circling miles away converged, as they lined up to face the parade ground, dead ahead. Within seconds, they turned their colored smoke on, and were rapidly closing in, as if aimed straight at us. This would need all our concentration as the noise built up. Just as the Cadet Captain stepped on the quarter deck at the end of his course, the planes thundered across overhead.

No feeling would come close to that moment.

One day, we got word that our Jagbir had, unknown to the rest of us, fought an aggressive cancer ... and sheathed his sword one last time. The man whose forearm could throw a javelin like a toothpick, was now embarking on his final journey. Most recently, in a landmark judgement, his death was ruled attributable to service causes, given that he was unable to get to a specialist hospital while being deployed at India's borders, and hence unable to leave.

RIP dear friend.... steady as she goes. Guard us from the skies.

CHAPTER 36 : SACHIN.... SACHIN

When cricketer Sachin Tendulkar made his debut in that Nov 1989 Karachi test, most of us 83rd National Defence Academy course types were weeks away from joining the Academy... A few remaining days of a First year college class (Khalsa College, Delhi University in my case) that we knew we would never complete, as we waited for the 'Joining Instructions' in brown UPSC envelope to show up, bearing the 3-lion emblem seal of the Govt of India.

Time was spent browsing the Tibetan market in Delhi buying stone-wash jeans, stocking up on grey, blue and white full sleeves shirts, and as soon as the booking window opened, we got our 1-way ticket on Jhelum Express to Pune.

Kapil Dev, the Captain who had led India to Prudential Cup victory in 1983 was coming to the tail end of his career, still putting in his 10-2-18-2 type stats and the inevitable collapse after his overs were done.. Shastri was never relatable, as being too much of a dandy - he was the guy your friend's sister had posters on her room walls, but for you, he wasn't a 'team player'.

The Mumbai versus rest of India camps were all too visible in Indian cricket

In his successes and triumphs, esp. over arch-enemy Pakistan, we found solace.. Be it as nascent 1st-termers (Wingies) lording over the ante room, or the dark days of 2nd term (*dukki* term) where an indulgent Senior would let us watch a match in the Squadron ante-room.

I remember 1999 as the year our course-mates proved their mettle at Kargil, and as the year Sachin came back to play - right after his father's death during the World Cup. That was something so very touching, so Academy-like in its 'get the job done' grit... so matter-of-fact.

Every Indian at that time can be deemed guilty of a bit of selfishness in hoping and praying for Sachin to come back to the tournament.

Some years later, the time came for Sachin to also hang up his boots, almost overlapping with our course hitting the mandatory 20-year service mark, making them pension-eligible and giving some the option to hang up their boots and camos and hit the civvy streets.

Mostly Olive Green parachutes - comfortable but not obscenely rich, would ensure their career transitions into a new innings on civilian street - while others will soldier on as the Services pyramid calls for greater efforts to scale ... Here's to an icon who TRULY captured our times in the 90s and the 'oughts'.

Associating with this Honorary Group Captain will be the mark of our times. God bless you Sachin. Long before India believed in itself, you made us believe in ourselves.

CHAPTER 37 - NOTE FROM HERE & THERE

Birth of the German Panzer Tank

As the Treaty of Versailles after the First World War prohibited Germany from having modern tanks, the few they had developed were also scrapped.

Incidentally, the British were the first to deploy WW 1 tanks against civilian workers on strike, to intimidate them - but in Glasgow, Scotland. Ironically, the city had raised the most money via 'tank bonds' to fund production of the very tanks lined against them.

A young German officer, Karl Hainz Guderian, soon began reading all he could find on tanks, and was considered good enough to be an authority on them, and began training the now-defeated German army, in tank warfare, by bolting tank outline cutouts on vehicles, and being able to maneuver their 'cannons'

But you cannot practice tank warfare without large open spaces - and none were to be found away from Allied supervision. The solution - the Germans turned to their enemies, the Russians, who had withdrawn from WW 1 after Lenin took over in the 1917 Revolution, and were in need of funding for the newly formed Soviet Union.

German giants Krupp, Rheinmetall and Daimler began producing what were called 'Gross tractors' and they were sent to Kazan, a city 800 km east of Moscow.

Soviet and German soldiers, together for the first time, began training - in Soviet uniforms, as part of a unit called KAMA. The money came from Germany, the space from Russia.

The Russians studied German tanks closely, and, by diverting funding from Germany, created another tank factory, which were initially mocked at for their simplicity. Many years would roll by, and the Russians would be known for their Guards Tank Armies, but they had a very humble beginning.

The Germans were happy with the first version of Panzer 1 - with a 34 km/h speed, and a great radio.

When an ailing Hindenburg died, Hitler became the Chancellor, and promptly canceled the KAMA program as he did not see the Soviets as allies. Stalin went a step further, imprisoning everyone and executing many of those talented tank men, who were a part of KAMA. This was also applied to Sniper school training between Germans and Russians, that was conducted at the Berlin Sniper School in the suburb of Zossen - and was alluded to in the movie 'Enemy at the Gates', where those Russians who trained as snipers with the Germans, were imprisoned and tortured for their possible support for Germany.

A good learning program for the Soviets was lost forever, and they would pay a heavy price when Operation Barbarossa would be launched by Hitler, as the tank corps had been decimated during Stalin's purges.

Leading the blitzkrieg into Russia in the 1941 summer would be the armored pincers led by Generals Hoth.... and Guderian, who would eventually make a pincer move- and capture Minsk, deep in Ukraine, and dooming 100s of 1,000s of poorly trained Soviets.

The Germans would improve the Mark 1 Panzer, eventually fielding the Mark 4, along with Tiger and Panther tanks, and be the most formidable tank corps till they were defeated in 1945. Guderian would survive the war, whereas Rommel would be forced by Hitler's henchmen to consume poison in the suppression of the von Stauffenberg briefcase bomb attack of Jul 20 1944 (role played by Tom Cruise in 'Valkyrie') - less than a year before WW 2 would come to an end in European theater.

Similar folly would be displayed by the Americans, who would turn down their radical new designs by an engineer named Christie - who would then export them to Russians, helping them create the BT tank, with a top speed of 80 km/hr

CHAPTER 38 - DOES THE BEST GENERAL LEAD IN WAR ?

Are modern armies the most egalitarian, best-man-for-the-role organization that safeguard national interests ? Allow me to elaborate

-Are Generals like Russia's Sergei Shoigu really the best leadership that a superpower could produce for a complex multi-pronged military offensive that Putin unleashed on Ukraine ?

-Why do straight-shooter Generals like Patton (US), Rommel (Germany) and Cariappa (India) end up being sidelined ?

-Is there an inherent aversion to hearing the truth within the decision-making process - civil and military alike ?

This is a tale of 2 Soviet Marshals of the Red Army battling the formidable German Wehrmacht during the Great Patriotic War, as the Russians describe the 1941-45 WW II war with Germany.

Marshal Georgy Zhukov's face would be mostly familiar as the liberator of Berlin. The other general would be a bit hard to recognize outside of avid military historians.

He is Marshal Ivan Konev, a 'soldier's soldier' molded in the Casimir Bodin mode of Tom Clancy war novels, and later, the architect of the suppression of Prague uprising, from which a young Andy Grove, the future co-founder of Intel escaped, to the safety of America.

A bit of context is in order...

The German Army during WW2 (Wehrmacht) was organized along Army Groups, the most famous of which being Army Group South, led by Field Marshal von Paulus, which reached, and based itself in the Ukrainian town of Zaporizhzhya, of nuclear-plant-under-shelling fame. (Note: It's not Chernobyl, this is in the south on the River Dnieper).

The Red Army was organized around 'Fronts', hence the names '1st Belorussian Front'. '1st Ukrainian Front', significantly manned by non-Russian, yet Soviet Socialist Republics (SSR) based ethnicities.

The battle theaters were named after the notable rivers the armies crossed, e.g. 'Don and Volga' in USSR, the Vistula in S Poland around Krakow, and then German-Polish border on the Oder-Neisse river, combined with the Bug-Mukhavets river on which stood the medieval fortress town of Brest-Litovsk, marking the Polish-Belorussian border.... which would play a significant role at the outset and closure of WW 2.After fighting and repulsing the Germans right from the pivotal Battle of Kursk, which remained the largest tank versus tank battle of WWII, Konev's armies liberated Odessa, Kharkiv and Kyiv, trapping and 'reducing' 1000s of German PoWs with Cossack horsemen swooping down with swords drawn on hapless prisoners.

Sometime in Spring, the Red Army stood poised to take the battle from occupied territories to German mainland, and eventually to Berlin. Like Konev, Marshall Zhukov had a strong leadership style, tactical acumen, and a long string of wins going back to the Russo-Japanese conflict of 1939 in Japanese-occupied Mongolia, which won him his first of many 'Hero of the Soviet Union' awards, ultimately commanding the 1st Belorussian Front - bringing him in direct contention with similarly-poised and illustrious Konev.

Who would Stalin give the singular honor of capturing Berlin, esp. after he had vetoed any Allied campaign for a similar move from the West towards Berlin ?

Stalin was paranoid by nature, surrounding himself with NKVD 'black operations' men, like Yagoda, Lavrenti Beria and others, each of whom falling out of favor and getting executed themselves. The Red Army purge of the 30s had left it bereft of capable generals, who would share honest appraisals of own and German capabilities, esp. in the false lull following the Molotov-Ribbentrop Pact carving up Poland between Germany and USSR. Konev's troops had both Ukrainian and Russians, but the Belorussians (White Russians) were deemed more pro-Soviet, something that continues to this date with Belarus being a ready supporter of Putin's War in Ukraine today.

Incidents of pockets of Ukrainians welcoming the German advance and possible toppling of Soviet hold on Ukraine had not gone unnoticed. A shared history of anti-Jewish pogroms over the centuries, led by Cossacks and expelling waves of Jews from Kiev, Kharkov, further bound the Ukrainians to the similarly disposed Germans.

Further, when Germany launched Operation Barbarossa, on June 22 1941, the tiny garrison in the riverine terrain resisted capture till late summer, with Red Army soldiers writing dying declarations in their own blood on the walls of the pulverized fortress.

A claim of loyalty to the USSR could not be more heroic, as Brest-Litovsk was granted a 'Hero City' status by Stalin.While Konev was well positioned to take the offensive into Germany, Stalin intervened, withholding approval. Similar to Hitler's folly in not capturing Dunkirk in 1940, and later keeping the approval for release of Panzer tank armies to himself, while the Allies established the Normandy beachhead in 1944, Stalin's intervention gave the retreating Wehrmacht time to dig in varying lines to resist the Soviet advance.

Konev's forces entered Berlin first, but Stalin gave Zhukov the honor of its capture and hoisting the Red Banner over the Reichstag. Konev was ordered to the south-west, where his forces linked up with elements of Patton's 8th Army, at Torgau and also retook Prague shortly after the official surrender of the German forces.

A preference for Belorussians over Ukrainians, and the reverberations of heroism of Brest-Litovsk defenders, defending Mother Russia, while away from mother Russia and from Belorussian soil, played a factor. No less were Zhukov's own people skills, letting Stalin be photographed with a large battle map, and a tape measure, happily playing along Stalin's own need for self-glorification.

True to form, Zhukov's win in 1945 brought cynosure and suspicion from Stalin, and in 1946, he was moved from being a counterpart to US's Gen Eisenhower, first to Odessa military district, then further back into the Urals, while an inquiry over war spoils was launched by Beria on Zhukov. The leadership of one of the pivotal 20th century battles was thus given on the basis of none-too-military aspects.

And such choices remain - v much a part of an organization's decision-making aspects.

CHAPTER 39 - WHEN YOUR COLLEGE WAS A FORMER ....

It's a known fact that Russian President Putin is a former KGB officer. The predecessor to KGB, was the NKVD, reporting directly to Stalin. For a time, 3 chiefs of NKVD were executed, with the successor often putting a bullet in the head of his former boss, and bringing his confession – often still wet with spittles of blood and saliva of the executed man – for Stalin's satisfaction.

Lavrenti Beria was the most well known NKVD chief, renowned for his sadism. Under him the NKVD even colluded with the Gestapo, and turned in several German and Austrian Communists to Gestapo, for immediate execution.

Caught up in all this were the Poles – trampled by the Germans from the west and the Soviets in the East. The division of Poland in the early 30s, was followed by various rounds of executions and purges of Polish military, aristocracy and anyone deemed to be capable of a position in the Polish state.

Stalin, with his penchant for deviousness, approved of the Katyn Forest massacres, where many 1,000s of Polish officers and troops were executed. Many of these executions were carried out using German submachine guns and pistols, thereby letting him declare the Nazis to be behind it, when ties between the 2 nations began to unravel and war seemed imminent.

In the mix is Vasily Blokhin, NKVD's specialist in 'wet operations' and assassinations. The NKVD held in its clutches, many 100s of survivors of Polish conquest, that needed to be dealt with. But the Katyn forest area was no longer under Soviet control.

Stalin, in Apr 1940, approved an order calling for execution of these Poles.

Wikipedia's entry on this shameful era best describes this...

"...Blokhin initially decided on an ambitious quota of 300 executions per night; and engineered an efficient system in which the prisoners were individually led to a small antechamber—which had been painted red and was known as the "Leninist room"—for a brief and cursory positive identification, before being handcuffed and led into the execution room next door.

The room was specially designed with padded walls for soundproofing, a sloping concrete floor with a drain and hose, and a log wall for the prisoners to stand against. Blokhin would stand waiting behind the door in his executioner garb: a leather butcher's apron, leather hat, and shoulder-length leather gloves. Then, without a hearing, the reading of a sentence or any other formalities, each prisoner was brought in and restrained by guards while Blokhin shot him once in the base of the skull with a German Walther Model 2 .25 ACP pistol. He had brought a briefcase full of his own Walther pistols, since he did not trust the reliability of the standard-issue Soviet TT-30 for the frequent, heavy use he intended. The use of a German pocket pistol, which was commonly carried by German police and intelligence agents, also provided plausible deniability of the executions if the bodies were discovered later."

An estimated 30 local NKVD agents, guards and drivers were pressed into service to escort prisoners to the basement, confirm identification, and post execution, remove the bodies and hose down the site. A sloping floor ensured quick drainage.

Although some of the executions were carried out by Senior Lieutenant of State Security Andrei Rubanov, Blokhin was the primary executioner and, true to his reputation, liked to work continuously and rapidly without interruption. In keeping with NKVD policy and the overall "wet" nature of the operation, the executions were conducted at night, starting at dark and continuing until just prior to dawn.

The bodies were continuously loaded onto covered flat-bed trucks through a back door in the execution chamber and trucked, twice a night, to Mednoye, where Blokhin had arranged for a bulldozer and two NKVD drivers to dispose of bodies at an unfenced site. Each night, 24–25 trenches, measuring 8x10 meters, were dug to hold that night's corpses, and each trench was covered up before dawn.

Blokhin and his team worked without pause for 10 hours each night, with Blokhin executing an average of one prisoner every three minutes. At the end of the night, Blokhin provided vodka to all his men.On 27 April 1940, Blokhin secretly received the Order of the Red Banner and a modest monthly pay premium as a reward from Joseph Stalin for his "skill and organization in the effective carrying out special tasks".His count of 7,000 shot in 28 days remains the most organized and protracted mass murder by a single individual on record and saw him being named the Guinness World Record holder for 'Most Prolific Executioner' in 2010.

Why am I telling this grim fact ?

While I had heard of Vasily Blokhin's wet works in Tver, it was inconceivable that after the years under Nazi and Soviet rule, any sign of such killings would have survived in the decades that followed. Unlike the Germans under Hitler, who were open about their killing of Jews, this was a diabolical plot against a neighbor's prisoners, without any whiff of it getting outside.

On a trip to Poland, I saw the 'Katyn Cross' put up prominently in Krakow, as a just way for a nation to seek closure.

I had read earlier that these executions happened in a city called Kalinnin, now renamed Tver. The NKVD headquarters functioned there from 1930-50. In 1954, per Soviet decree – in an almost routine move – a dentistry school, followed by a medical school were set up here 'Tver State Medical Academy' with a good enrollment, faculty, and accepting students from India, Middle East and all over the world.

This was my wife's Medical college. In a time when Western education was costly, the Soviets offer to train Indian students in medicine and engineering, causing many students to learn Russian, and get access to quality education that was rare and expensive in the early 90s.

When we went visiting the campus, the doors to the basement were locked.They still conduct anatomical dissections in the basement, along with offices of some of the faculty, and lecture halls. Outside the main building, I saw 2 plaques, very ordinary looking – one in Russian, another in Polish. The Russian one simply stated :

'in memory of those oppressed here from 1930-50, at this location of NKVD HQ for Tver Oblast (province).'

The Polish one showed a cross with human hands wrapped by barbed wire at its base , an insignia of prisoners, and identical to the art seen at the Katyn Cross.

Instantly, it all came together.

This was the building where NKVD had its HQ for the Tver Oblast (province). This building would have a sloping execution chamber in its basement. Up top, the unmistakable Soviet Hammer and Sickle logo stood, whitewashed. I could make out that the name of the college, while in cement, was of a different material, and seemed to be added much later on.

The timeline of the college's move (1954) is subsequent to NKVD's wrapping up its business of death here, around 1950. It all added up that this was the place where Vassily Blokhin shot 7,000 Polish prisoners over 28 nights.

Later, I was to get confirmation from a local that this was indeed the place where NKVD killed 'thousands'.

As the day of our visit coincided with Admissions day, the college had many prospective applicants in its halls. If only they knew about its past. But then, it was no fault of the college, and at least its building was now being put to a better use.

Its past, **IN NO WAY**, besmirches the college.

They themselves are a victim of this unfortunate saga.

After all, at India's King Edward Medical College in Lucknow, and the 'Machlee Mahal' where the British, in an act of vengeance lasting years after the 1857 Mutiny, continued to hang, daily, many batches of Indians, for about 3 years, without stop. Those buildings are now put to similar use.

But this saga only seems sinister by its silence, and its near normalcy. For it is no less sinister than the gas chamber remains at Birkenau, the surviving execution wall at Auschwitz and the remains of Gestapo's HQ at Berlin.

Sadly, the Soviets, and now the Russians would not allow the Polish Govt to commemorate their dead, or give them even a single room in the building. The plaque, visible only if you are looking for it, are all that are there, lost and forlorn like the souls that got consumed here.

They are the real victims here.

CHAPTER 40. FAREWELL 'FISHBED"

On Sep 26th 2025, the Indian Air Force (IAF) bid adieu to the MiG-21 fighter aircraft (NATO code-name : Fishbed), one of its most storied warplanes that has inspired reverence, respect and fear alike.

I have had the honor of knowing some of the finest exponents of MiG flying - some have nationwide fame for scribbling Bollywood dialog in chalk on bombs ready to be dropped in the icy heights of Olthingthang and Kargil, during the 1999 conflict. During our NDA training, we had the cream of the IAF posted as our Instructors, with the senior lot having seen action during the 1971 War.

Back in the heat of 1994, my T-72 tank unit was deployed along the Suratgarh - Fort Abbas Sector, as part of India's Strike Corps annual exercise 'Bhavani Khadka'. It was the end of Day 2 of a 3 day 'advance to contact' type maneuvre in the Rajasthan desert. Me and my Troop Leader, a Lt, had dismounted from the tanks to help the crewmen with their replenishment tasks.

'All stations Bravo-Sierra-Golf ... F-16 cluster attack approaching', or words to that effect came over the radio net, with the distinctive call-sign of the Commandant of our unit.

'What the ...' 'Is this for real..?'
We looked at each other, as we leaped back onto our tanks. Earlier in the day, we had seen the Air Force conduct mock strafing and rocketing runs at other unit's tanks and BMPs, and then the 'A-Ha' moment struck us.

The drill called for warplanes to simulate their own tank attack procedures. We, the intended targets, were to man the 12.7 mm (50-cal in US parlance) NSVT Air Defense Machine Gun, and aim back and mock-fire at the warplanes through our gun-sights.

The crescendo and cacophony grew as tanks jockeyed and the planes swooped in like silver birds of prey. A formation of 4 MiG 21s came in blindingly fast, out of the setting sun - just as a F16 attack would unfold, hiding in the sun's glare. About 2-3 km away, still barely audible, they rocketed skywards, and then from the apogee of the curve at about 5-6,000 ft- they began their dive, aiming for the tanks around me.

The last MiG aimed straight at my tank. I desperately tried to keep it within the cross-hairs, and simulated the electric firing trigger. I resisted the temptation to bring up my puny Hot Shot camera and take a pic - for good reason. It was all over in a matter of 5-6 seconds. Later, at the debrief, a pic would flash before a 1,000 officers - taken from the camera gun of a MiG, capturing another camera - not the NSVT - aimed back at it. A gross violation of laid down counter fire drills. Expletives followed.

31 years later, as the Air Chief would say, 'we don't drive 50 year old cars, but we fly 50 year old planes.' So goodbye old friend, and thanks for flying countless CAPs to protect the Pongos deployed in the mountains and deserts below.

CHAPTER 41. BRUSH WITH GREATNESS

Bollywood's biopic 'Ikkees' (21) is about to hit the box office - a tale of valor of 2/Lt Arun Khetarpal, a young cavalry officer of the storied Poona Horse, who died at that age in the Battle of Basantar river on Dec 16 1971, and awarded India's highest military battle honor, the Param Vir Chakra. Fittingly, the motif of the medal is the Vajra weapon of Lord Indra, built from the femoral bones of Rishi Dadhichi, who sacrificed himself to fashion a weapon to take down the demon Vritra.

Being one of the youngest to be awarded for his ultimate sacrifice, Arun's valor and martyrdom resonates a lot with my course.We have coursemates, whose fathers died in combat, without having met their sons, who followed in their footsteps. Others have dads who have led with conspicuous bravery, such as at the ferocious Battle of Pul Kanjari (the Dancing girl's bridge).

For me, Arun's education at Lawrence School Sanawar, a school founded by my Regiment's founder, Maj Hodson, and alma mater to the who's who of Bollywood, and Indian industry.Further, with him being from NDA's Foxtrot Squadron, called 'Khetarpal's Fortress' made him a stylish near-peer to emulate, for us in Echo squadron.

Both during 1965 and 1971 wars, Hodsons Horse and Poona Horse have led India's armoured response, fighting in the Lahore and Jammu theatres, so the bond between the 2 regiments is storied, deep and multi-generational. During the battle, Hodson's tankmen working in tandem with Arun's troop, fought pitched battles with enemy's 13th Lancers, equipped with US-supplied M48 Patton tanks, in an hours long battle fought in an anti-tank minefield.

Hodson's Horse famously disregards minefields as a tank obstacle to this day, showing how a single mine can be encountered across a 1000 m deep minefield, and would rather sacrifice a tank, than stop its move.

While in my 4th term, I was bored glancing through official precis, reading up for an exam. These booklets are issued for the term, and often have initials and academy numbers of prior cadets to who they were issued to. Perhaps the present day Academy Cadet Adjutant, or one of our Directing Staff's names would pop up.

Within NDA, the 'Fable of 19' was a thing those days, meaning, the 19th NDA course went to war with China in 1962, its double, the 38th course - Arun's course - fought in 1971, and given the worsening counter-insurgency blowing up in late 80s Kashmir, the next 'double' the 76th course was believed to be destined for war, around 1989, at a time when the Army was fighting pitched battles in the Kashmir valley, and artillery duels on the Line of control.

That day, a tightly written ballpoint text caught my eye - Arun Khetrapal/his Academy number/F/38. It was as if a jolt ran through my body. I called my neighbor to share what I had found. We looked at each other. Sometime during 68-69, this precis was with the cadet whose life size portrait adorned the lobby of the Sudan Block. The one for whom NDA's Parade Ground is named. In an instant, his eternal immortality reached out to my ordinary cadet life,as though reassuring me that deep down, we all shared the same bond. That he too must have been bored stiff being required to master the contents of the precis, failing which relegation was always a slow-march away.

For many days, I kept the precis open at that page. Daydreaming in the pre-internet era. The river bed lined with rounded rocks. The sugarcane and sarkandaa fields that were set on fire by both armies. The close range at which tank-versus-tank battles were fought.I dont mind confessing that I thought of retaining the precis forever, paying the fine instead. But that would be a cisservice to the future courses of cadets, who would otherwise be denied that charge that I experienced.

At the end of the course, while handing over the issued books and precis back, I held on to its weathered binding one last time. Giving it up with a reverence deserved of Gods.Hope it continues to inspire future batches the same way it gave me a brush with greatness.